To outwit the fate

by

K. E. Adamus

161 DAYS

Prologue

I'm in prison, and I'll tell you honestly - I'm not happy about free meals and a roof over my head. Of course, I'm innocent and not in the same sense as half of the prisoners. Most swear at the ashes of loved ones that they did not commit the crimes they were accused of. The other prisoners are proud of their actions. I'm really innocent, but the court ruled otherwise. What does the truth look like? Judge for yourself!

Robots won't give you money!

To succeed, you need to be in the right place at the right time with the right product for sale. I was always in the worst possible circumstances. With my head bowed, I waited for my "Damocles sword", and instead of products, I carried the status of an individual experienced by fateful events.

On sunny days, I always found my feet in muddy puddles of a suspicious color and smell. On rainy days, umbrellas turned inside out and mocked me with broken wires. When I had scheduled essential tasks, the alarm did not ring, and I overslept most of my life events. When something nice happened, it aroused reasonable concern immediately. Maybe good events were just a prelude to some fatal situation in which I would lose the remains of my dignity?

Not wanting to play with fate, I hid at home and made small robots out of metal screws and plates. It took me all through high school to figure out how to create a self-propelling mechanism to make the robots move from time to time. I wanted to sell a few clones of my favorite prototype to my colleagues.

"These are puppets, not robots." My friends were clear about their opinions. "Robots do something, and yours can only move from time to time with a limb."

Being bitter, which was also due to fatal grades in mathematics and physics, I gave up my engineering career.

"You won't make money on screws!" my parents kept telling me every time I forgot to come to dinner, because I was working on another project.

This experience has taught me one thing – I will never earn on my passion. I had a lot of time to think. At that time, there was no public Internet available. One of my dreams was independence. I wanted to have my own money. The road to wealth rarely goes through the generally respected scheme: master's degree and work, but I didn't know that yet. I wanted special skills to help me find a job anytime, anywhere - regardless of time and place. Bemused by the widely propagated scheme, I did not go to technical college but to high school. Here I learned more details about the construction of the paramecium. I still didn't have any skills that would allow me to become independent. I didn't aim high. I just wanted to have my own money and replicate the generally promoted lifestyle - a once-a-year vacation and work for my home mortgage and future family needs.

After graduating high school, I still had time to verify this matrix. However, I decided to go to college and play with my fate. At eighteen, I was not attracted to any of the fields of study taught at universities and colleges. I found it worth taking care of myself in such a case and doing some self-analysis.

I was about to become a psychologist, set up my own office, and earn a lot of money, but I overslept and missed the train that was supposed to take me to the exam for psychological studies. I did a quick review of the other subjects of study to which I could still submit papers. I ended up in a nearby city, engaging in cultural studies. To my surprise, I passed the first semester without any problems and found the theories fascinating. I had already imagined myself as a professor of cultural studies, going to foreign seminars and publishing several scientific books every year. Obviously, I saw myself as an author of wonderful books that can change the course of history.

That was until one day in May when I decided to buy truffle chocolates. The nearby store was dominated by pies, frankfurters, and fake chocolate products, so I decided to go to a supermarket on the city's outskirts. Of course, I forgot the monthly ticket and was fined by the controllers on the tram. This did not spoil my mood. Since something unpleasant had already happened, the rest of the day should be idyllic. It was not.

At the supermarket, a young child, eating a caramel bar he probably stole, vomited on me. Fortunately, the secretions did not reach the chocolates. I went to the most distant cash register to pass unnoticed through the supermarket, pay and clean my soiled clothes in the toilet. Two people stood at the cash register.

I stood shyly behind them, feeling I stunk off the kid's digestive juices. After reading thousands of thrillers, I always thought I was the perfect candidate for a spy, as I have a great sense of observation and perception. In fact, it took me two minutes to realize that one of my lecturers, doctor Plonski, was standing in line. I wanted to greet him politely, but the woman with him asked him first:

"Are you also buying your wife lard for dinner?"

"No, I'm buying her a mortadella," answered Dr. Plonski.

I was wondering what I should be most embarrassed about: the fact that I met the lecturer in my vomit-covered clothes (there was no sign that it was someone else's vomit, and the lecturer could think that it was my own), that I met the lecturer with his mistress or that I spotted him with lack of class. His lover definitely deserved a ham.

Doctor Plonski did not share the mastery of perceptiveness either because only then he saw me.

"You will pay for shopping..." he said to his mistress and ran out of the supermarket.

"I think I'll dump him," the lover sighed to the cashier. "It was supposed to be a romantic dinner for two, and he buys lard, black pudding, and "supermarket" brand beer."

"You should pay fifty-five zloty." the cashier replied.

"So much?"

"If you can't afford it, sweetheart, there will be no romantic dinner!" The cashier apparently did not tolerate betrayal.

The doctor's mistress dug out the money from her purse. She handed the cashier a hundred-zloty banknote in a gesture of presenting her hand to kiss. Amused, I waited for the cashier's next move. She did not disappoint me. She took out a marker pen and checked whether the banknote was forged. Without a word, she gave the change, ignoring the woman's outstretched hand and spilling money on the tray.

She scanned my chocolates without waiting for the doctor's lover to collect the money.

"It would be better to spend that money on laundry," she said without returning my smile.

I decided not to tell anyone about doctor Plonski's affair. Keeping my secret, I felt like a 100% gentleman. Also, I've never dealt with gossip, considering it offensive to my dignity.

Unfortunately, doctor Plonski did not know about this. He probably assumed that news about his lover was broadcasted even on student radio. He devoted his first lecture after the unfortunate meeting to the topic of betrayal.

For an hour and a half, he described the social and cultural inclinations of betrayal in various countries and among diverse ethnic groups. He quoted funny anecdotes, proverbs, and numerous quotes. The students laughed and whispered comments among themselves about the lecture.

"Faithfulness is a strong itch with the prohibition of scratching" - doctor Plonski finished his lecture, quoting Julian Tuwim. He quickly gathered his things and left the hall without waiting for the students' questions.

During the lecture, I had the impression that the lecturer was watching me. I didn't feel comfortable with it. I waited anxiously for the final oral exam. As it turned out, the fear was justified.

On the day of the exam, bad luck faithfully accompanied my meager person. After celebrating his successful passing of the course's exam, the roommate, with a hangover, poured a pot of baked beans on my prepared suit. Only the pants survived. The jacket was suitable for three rounds of dry cleaning. The other clothes were wet after successfully accessing the washing machine in the dorm. An embarrassed roommate pulled his XXL blue sweater with a pink diamond pattern out of the closet. Nolens volens, I put on this monstrous sweater and ran for the exam.

I was third in line to check my knowledge. Doctor Plonski ignored my greeting, ordered me to sit down, and asked the first question.

"Please tell me, based on your knowledge, about the cultural conditions of the rumor."

"So the rumors unite social groups." I began maneuvering through the maze of information gained from the lecture and read in the past scientific publications. "They can constitute successful interpersonal communication.

Sometimes they can even turn into anecdotes and, for example, urban legends..."

"Wrong," the lecturer interrupted, "You talk about the effects and role of gossip all the time, and I asked about the cultural conditions of their creation. Let's move on to the next question. Please talk about betrayal in African tribes; I saw you..."

"I was just buying chocolates!" I interrupted.

"I don't know anything about chocolates," answered the doctor. "I saw you, you were at this lecture, so the question should be straightforward."

From the information about the African tribes, I only remembered the one about the Hotatots' steatopygia, so I stayed silent, terrified, without even trying to improvise.

"The last question," doctor Plonski broke the onerous silence, "Please, give me a definition of socialization on the example of Polish Tatars."

"Before answering the question, I will tell an anecdote about the invention of a dish called Tatar..." I began to describe the adventures of a raw chop under Tatar saddle when the doctor interrupted me.

"You're raving. I hope that you will be better prepared for the retake exam."

I left the room devastated. With a high score from previous exams, I was counting on a scholarship, but apparently, bad luck had only gone on a few months' vacations, and now it was working with doubled energy.

"You traitor!" I cursed at the doctor. I wanted to tell everyone about his affair, but after failing the exam, I became unreliable. I regretted my gentleman's discretion.

"Another top score?" Alice asked.

I didn't want to talk to her. I liked her in the first class when I watched her athletically built body, but the charm lasted until she turned and I saw her face. She was ugly; her dun, small eyes, beaked nose, and wide face effectively discouraged me.

Unfortunately, this animosity did not work the other way. Alice apparently fell in love with me. She kept bringing me lunch, lending lecture notes, and always tried to sit in the next seat in the class.

She was intelligent and had extensive knowledge. Conversations with her could improve the mood of each interlocutor. It bothered me. If only she would understand that we can only be buddies. Her courtship prevented me from making friends with Monica. Despite the jet-black hair, Monica behaved like a dumb blonde from jokes. Still, her beauty charmed all students so much that they forgave her mental deficiencies.

"So, how did it go?" Alice repeated the question.

"I failed." I wanted to give my speech a nonchalant tone, but my voice let me down, and only a thin squeal escaped my throat.

"It's probably because of that Masonic sweater," I heard the sweetest voice of the year.

It was Monica who interrupted our conversation. Immediately, my zest came back. *She's so funny; maybe she pretends to be silly,* I thought. *Maybe this is my few seconds' chance to get her attention.*

"Well, if I go through the next stage in the lodge, I'll certainly pass all the subjects, even without going to lectures," I continued with a smile.

"Until then, you will fill in this too-big sweater and it will destroy itself from walking in it every day," Monica smiled sweetly.

Other students standing nearby began to laugh. No retort came to mind, so I began to laugh, immediately self-effacing.

"It probably won't happen," I said. "I'll gain weight, so the sweater will become too tight, and I will walk in another one."

Alice grabbed my loosely hanging sleeve and pulled me aside.

"You could have a little more dignity," she began to rebuke me. "Don't let some small brains bully you, even if they are set in a beautiful face."

"She was definitely joking," I began to defend myself. "Besides, you must have a distance to yourself, right?"

"You would forgive her even if she poured a bucket of cesspool water over you." "How do you know?"

"That's it. I just saw a sample of this activity," Alice sighed and took me for a coffee at a nearby cafe.

In case of failing the first exam, it was still possible to take two others - the retake ones. Throughout the holidays, I sat over the notes and read academic readings not to give doctor Plonski satisfaction during the retake exam. I interrupted my education only to pick up one of the robots neglected during my studies.

I arrived in the dorm on the eve of the first retake exam date. I preferred to pay for accommodation and be sure I would be on time. I read my notes until 3 a.m. Finally, tired, I set the alarm clock and went to sleep. My roommate was still studying for the organic chemistry retake exam.

The next day, I woke up with a strange sense of defeat. Something was wrong. It was a beautiful September day outside, and it looked like it was noon, not morning. I jumped up, terrified. Next to my alarm clock were its batteries and a card from my roommate.

"I'm sorry, but the alarm clock is ticking too loudly, and I can't focus on science."

I could hardly read the doodle of a future chemist. My alarm on the cell phone didn't ring either. I dressed quickly and ran to the university. Doctor Plonski was already gone. I waited two hours in the queue at the secretary's office. When my turn finally came, stuttering, I explained the situation.

The secretary told me to write an application for the next exam date. It took me a few minutes to fill in the application, but I had to wait in line again.

"Did you know that the first retake exam date is already over?" the secretary said after reading the application.

"It's because of that chemistry student," I began to defend myself.

"Please be prepared for the fact that, as a humanist, you will lose any battle with engineers' kind of minds!" said the secretary and with a loud, "Thank you, that's all!" let me know that the audience in the secretariat is over.

After a week, a letter came with a new exam date. However, bad luck did not let go. My godfather died. On the day of the exam I went to the funeral. I asked my godfather's wife for a copy of the death certificate to present the document at the university and explain why I didn't attend the exam again. She murmured something about the desirability of the inheritance, commenting on my request, and it ended there.

Soon a letter about my removal from the student list came. My parents knew nothing about these problems, and I wanted it to stay that way. They were poor, and I knew that my studies seriously affected the household budget.

I decided to write a letter to the provost of the university. I described the meeting with doctor Plonski and his lover, I just didn't remember what they were buying, and I wrote about the headcheese in the letter. The answer came quickly.

In abusive words, the rector informed me that he personally knows doctor Plonski, who is allergic to headcheese. Besides, he is an exemplary husband and father. The rector wrote that he could take the case to court for alleged slander.

In the end, he added that I had a "wolf ticket", which in Poland meant a lifelong ban on studying at his university. In this way, my attempt to become independent, using generally respected tricks, that is, study, study, and then work full-time, ended in failure. However, I wasn't going to give up

Your baccalaureate won't give you a job!

I concealed my defeat from my family. At the end of September, I packed my stuff and pretended to attend university. Earlier, Alicia had agreed to let me live with her in the dormitory. She had a single room, a privilege rarely available to second year students. However, Alicia got extra points for working on the dormitory residents' board and being an orphan.

"My parents abandoned me because I was ugly."

She sometimes felt sorry for herself after drinking too much alcohol. Usually, I didn't know how to respond to such exaggerations. If I had said she wasn't ugly, I would have lied. Her ugliness would have been confirmed if I had said it was for another reason. That's why I murmured under my nose that everything would be okay and patted her on the back.

Alicia asked one of her colleagues from the residents' board to issue me with a student dormitory card. At the entrance of the building, a bodyguard wandered around in the evenings. He took advantage of the students out of frustration with his unfulfilled ambition to pass the secondary school exams.

The guests of the residents had to leave their identity documents at the reception desk, and if they did not have a card signed by the residents' board, they had to pay several dozen zlotys for their stay when they left the dormitory after midnight. That's why I needed an actual permanent resident card. A few days after moving into Alicia's room, I went to the Employment Office to register as unemployed.

"You do not come under our authority," said the agency worker. "Please go to the district office where you are a permanent resident."

I tried to beg the woman, but she was not impressed by my experience and descriptions of life disasters.

"If you are unlucky, you won't be able to prove yourself at work anyway," she said and screamed: "Next!" towards the queue.

With a strange feeling in my stomach, I left the building after checking the noticeboard. They were looking for a welder, electrician, and baker. Nobody was looking for unemployed high school graduates. For a moment, I remembered my dream to possess the skills that would help me find a job everywhere and anytime. Why didn't I become a super electrician?

A beautiful October day was not a time to get depressed with its transparent air, golden and purple leaves of trees in parks and on the streets, and slanted rays of sunshine. It was certainly not the perfect weather for suicides.

However, just in case, I brewed St. John's wort, which has a slightly antidepressant effect. I could not afford despair and self-pity. After drinking the infusion, I felt an influx of energy, although I felt like I was under some intoxicating substance.

I ran downstairs to an internet cafe (Alicia had her laptop secured with a password), and full of inspiration, I started to write a brief resume.

I skipped a year of studying to avoid employers asking questions about my failure, and instead, I extended my distribution of leaflets and advertising material by a year. I added a photo from the mountains, in which my athletic figure looked nice. My face, with dark hair and green eyes, looked handsome because of the small number of pixels; no one could see the few pimples that always blemished my face.

I then registered on the job search portal and sent my CV to fifty different places. I applied for a waiter, sales representative, call center employee, security guard, and chef's assistant positions. I always made good scrambled eggs. Satisfied, I returned to Alicia's room.

My friend had just come back from class. When I saw her, she looked at me with a confused face.

"Tell me right away what happened," I asked.

"Terrible rumors are spreading about you. Everyone says you didn't pass, despite easy questions, and that you're too stupid to study."

"In a year, I'll be passing the exams on economics or law or psychology. Now, I have to find a job because I won't get a student loan this year."

"You are intelligent. You will surely find something."

"Intelligent people are looking for jobs with the required higher education. I don't have the qualifications now; I just need anything."

As it turned out, finding "just about anything" wasn't so easy, especially since bad luck didn't let me go. I sent fifty different applications every day, but the phone remained silent.

Only after two weeks, I was called with an offer to work on sorting product elements in a nearby factory. I put on a suit and a blue shirt - because it is said that blue color has some effect and most entrepreneurs and politicians wear it. I put my only Gore-Tex jacket on top of that and headed to the meeting.

The sporty coat didn't correspond well with my elegant outfit, so I took it off two blocks from the factory building and put it in a bag. A few steps later, I felt a smack on my shoulder. It was a flying pigeon that had released its droppings on me.

I cursed all the gods and was going to condemn them for several generations back and forth, but I got a little lost and looped because of my lack of knowledge about gods of all kinds. I was in a hurry.. I did not have a handkerchief. They were in the backpack, which I usually carried with me. So I appeared shitty and stinky for the interview.

"Lucky you," the obese lady from the HR department tried to joke, but her crooked face suggested my candidacy would not be considered. "Unfortunately, we've already filled all the vacancies," she said after a while.

"Then why didn't anyone cancel the meeting?" I was outraged.

"I do not like your attitude," she replied, "There are jobs in advertising waiting for rebels, but you do not have the proper education and skills for that. Please work on yourself."

"And I suggest you practice your posture through gymnastics. It would be useful to lose a few dozen kilograms, so your spine can rest," I answered.

Rarely have I been so nasty, but I felt that I had come to the end of allowing myself to be disregarded. I didn't know this was only the beginning of more perverse events and my dignity and honor would be irretrievably lost.

"Goodbye," she said. "At least I don't have to wear a bird poo on myself."

I felt that I had lost my voice due to emotions, so I couldn't muster any retort, and the woman triumphantly watched my back as I departed. A few minutes later, the phone rang. It turned out that it was about a job in a call center.

Unfortunately, my voice still has not returned to normal.

"Yes, I would be happy to work after hours," I squeaked into the handset.

"Unfortunately, your voice does not sound trustworthy. Is it a mutation? How old are you?"

"Temporary sore throat." I tried to defend myself.

"You have a problem with your throat so early in the autumn? This does not bode well," said my interlocutor and hung up.

"Fucking hell."

"What's the problem?" I heard behind me.

I turned around and saw a monk. I did not know anything about monk's uniforms, so it was difficult initially to know who I was dealing with.

So the messenger of God was standing in front of me. I could devour him without consequences; he would turn the other cheek.

"I am looking for a job, and your God is interfering with that. He is an incarnate evil!" I started my speech with a squeaky voice.

"The paths of the Lord are not being explored," answered the religious man.

"I am not a believer, but if God exists and you are his messenger, the world is in a bad situation," I said.

Considering the conversation to be over, I began to move on.

"We also have many non-believers," continued the monk.

"Is this some kind of hidden camera?" I asked him, confused.

"This is my business card." He gave me a piece of paper. "When you are ready, call me."

"Why do I need a faggot's business card!"

His quick punch to my jaw confused me a little.

"Shit!" I said in shock. It was the only word I could think of. The monk left with a springy step without looking back.

I picked up the business card from the sidewalk and dropped it into the bag.

"Show it, show it!" Alicia tormented me two hours later.

"Brother Edgar's spiritual advice," she read out loud when I handed her the card.

"Maybe I'll join the monastery for a year?" I started to fool around, hiding my resentment and the insult to honor behind jokes. I couldn't even fight. "Food and accommodation for free. And I'll probably learn boxing."

"They will lock you up and not let you go."

"I'll grow a beard, memorize motivational talk and become a monk guru."

My jokes didn't even make sense to me. I couldn't stay with Alicia all the time; someone could report my presence, and she would have problems.

The next day I was woken up by a phone ringtone in the morning. A lovely lady called with an offer of a job in security. I confirmed that I knew the intervention techniques, and she arranged a meeting with the boss the next day.

Satisfied, I put my cell phone away. And suddenly the phone started to ring and ring. They called about various offers, from sales representatives to administrators, and they all wanted to make an appointment at the same time as the lady in charge of security.

"Unfortunately, I can't make it tomorrow. I am taking my colleague to the airport," I lied.

"We are looking for available people. Those who put work before their personal life," I heard every time.

After answering eleven calls, I turned off my cell phone and dug into my sleeping bag. The bed in the room was only one meter wide, and despite Alicia's suggestion to sleep on it together, I preferred a sleeping bag and a mattress on the floor.

I sent a text message to Alicia: "Does shit happen for a reason or not for a reason?"

"What happened this time? Were you robbed by some great-grandmother?" she wrote back.

"All employers want me to multiply my person and simultaneously go to several job interviews."

"I'll buy wine. That's a good sign."

I have become Alice's keeper, I thought.

Recently she had been buying food for both of us and cooking dinners in a shared kitchen on the first floor. She also left me some change for coffee in the city when I was distributing my poor resume to all kinds of institutions.

"I think it's time for me to write to Brother Edgar and ask the Holy Spirit to intercede so I can be in several places simultaneously," I replied.

"Brother Edgar fancies your legs."

The next day, freshly shaved and smelling Alice's unisex perfume, I went for an interview. I woke up on time and caught the bus... and the bad luck started.

A woman started giving birth on the bus. The driver stopped the vehicle and waited for the ambulance. I got off and wanted to call a taxi, but my mobile phone refused to cooperate. After dialing the number, there was only noise, and I couldn't make the call. I tried to borrow a phone from someone, but everyone answered in the negative, without even listening to my explanation. After half an hour, another bus arrived. Unfortunately, I arrived too late at my destination.

"The next candidates are being interviewed now. And by the way, this lack of punctuality is a bad sign of the candidate," said the receptionist.

She was not moved by my stories about the woman giving birth.

"That's how everyone explains themselves. If they were telling the truth about all these births, we would have a real baby boom," she said.

After leaving the building, I felt that I had to defraud the change for coffee from Alicia. I entered an academic pub and ordered a beer. Then another one. And another one. A newspaper with advertisements was lying on the table. I started to browse through the offers, and suddenly my gaze stopped on one of the announcements.

"I will pay for male companionship. 250 zlotys per hour of conversation," it read.

If I talked and talked or listened for three hours, I would earn a month's rent for a room. I started to calculate. But probably the same person doesn't spend so much money in the same way, so maybe I'll place an advertisement.

After drinking alcohol, I did various ill-considered things, and placing an advertisement via SMS about being able to provide escort services was one of those things.

"A handsome twenty-year-old will talk to you, listen to you, pretend to be your boyfriend in front of your friends."

I didn't mention anything about sex and decided to explain it every time I talked to potential clients over the phone. The announcement was supposed to be published in a new newspaper issue in the next few days. Buzzed up after a few beers, I decided not to wait a few days for the Eldorado but to call about the conversation for 250 zlotys.

"What advertisement?" my cell phone worked, but the interlocutor didn't know what was happening. "It must have been my friends who tricked me. And how much do I supposedly pay? 250 zlotys? Come and see me, sweetie. I'm already preparing coffee!"

I was stressed out by this conversation, but I decided not to give up. The address was in the city center, close to the pub. Fifteen minutes later, I pressed the bell at the door of the tenement house.

"Is that you, sweetheart? Please come in."

The woman had a pleasant voice, which did not announce the sight of a gorgon, which appeared to me three minutes later. She weighed about 200 kilograms, placed in tight leggings. The t-shirt stained with food showed that the owner was without a bra.

"It's only a conversation," I started to repeat the mantra in my mind, also losing about 50 percent of the respect I still had for myself.

"Show me, sweetheart, the announcement," she said. "My name is Aneta. Ha ha ha... Two hundred and fifty zlotys per hour of conversation. So, honey, what are we going to talk about?"

"Would you like to talk about everything to me?" I suggested. "I guess you're lonely..."

"Where did you get these ideas from? Why do you think so?" she leaned her hands on her fat hips.

"Otherwise, my friends would not have placed an advertisement," I guessed that talking about her obesity wouldn't bring a friendly atmosphere to the conversation.

"Maybe that's right. Wait a moment; I'll bring the cake to the coffee."

After ten minutes of Aneta's absence, I thought she might have fainted, and I wanted to go to rescue her when she appeared naked at the door. Her legs were unshaven, and her bikini area was bushy too. She touched her blonde hair with black roots with her hand and said:

"Well, get ready, sweetheart, because I won't pay for the conversation."

"I'm a virgin, so you understand," I lied.

"I don't mind at all."

"This first time must be magical."

"Hocus-pocus," she answered with an old joke. "Is that enough?"

"No!"

I grabbed my bag and started running. Naked Aneta started chasing me up the stairs.

"Come back. You haven't earned anything yet!" She didn't run out into the street, but I was rushing further towards the dormitory door with a traumatic image of naked Aneta written in my subconscious mind.

I didn't tell Alicia about my gigolo excesses. It wasn't something to share with a person in love with you. A few days later, she raised the subject herself.

"I saw your ad!"

My phone number was printed in the announcement. Most of my friends didn't even remember their mobile phone numbers, so I felt safe. Unfortunately, clearly, Alicia knew my number by heart.

"This is not going to be a bad thing," I started to defend myself. "No sex, just talking and pretending to be a boyfriend in front of friends or co-workers of a given person."

"You value yourself cheaply."

"What, am I not counting enough?" I made a joke.

"And what were you looking for in social advertisements?"

"I want to write a scientific paper on gigolos."

"I can provide you with some material," I told her about Aneta with details.

"A gigolo virgin is a bit of a stretch..."

The conversation was interrupted by an incoming SMS on my mobile phone.

"I am interested in your offer. There's a long engagement at stake. Meet me at the cafe to discuss the details. Greetings, Pelagia."

I showed Alicia the message. Her face turned red with emotion.

"You really can't find a normal job?"

"I've been looking for it for a month now. I would prefer a regular job myself, but as you can see, bad luck doesn't give up. I can't stay with you because your neighbors already know I'm staying here. You may have problems." I replied to a text message and set up a meeting in a cafe rarely frequented by students, far from a student town.

I put on a suit and a beige shirt I had received for my birthday last year from Alicia. She noticed this and looked upset.

"It's just a reconnaissance," I started explaining.

Alicia did not answer. She took out a can of beer from the fridge. I saw she was in a bad mood, but I didn't have time.

I ran out of the room and rushed to the cafe. Pelagia said she was blonde and would be dressed in black. I went into the restaurant and saw a few blondes in black dresses sitting alone at tables.

"It's some kind of sponsor ladies' gathering," I thought, assessing their age at forty to fifty. One of the women waved her hand towards me.

She looked about fifty years old, but she was well groomed and beautiful. Oxidized blonde hair did not show a single centimeter of roots. Gentle make-up, green eyes... Why is this woman looking for a gigolo?

"Mrs. Pelagia?" I came up intimidated.

"Darling, how old are you? Not too early for such a job?"

I sat down at the table and briefly told my story of the last few months.

"I think I can help you," she said.

In exchange for an hour spent together every day, she offered a room with food in her apartment and a small allowance. She did not require sexual services, which I wanted to believe in.

After her husband's death, she felt lonely. She was childless and had no close family or friends in the city. She thought about offering some company to a friendly female student but was afraid of accusations of homosexuality. I couldn't believe my happiness. Didn't the lousy luck let it go?

"What's the catch?" I asked.

"It is a little bizarre but harmless," said Pelagia. "During this time spent together, you must wear a mask."

In my thoughts, I remembered various masks from thrillers and felt a bit strange.

"I made the mask two years ago," continued Pelagia. "It's my face, two years younger. It may signify oddity and vanity, but I'd like to see myself when I was a little younger. This will create a certain mood for conversation."

"I'm in," I've decided. I wanted to pray in my thoughts, but I remembered that I had a private war with a god or gods. If they existed, it was better not to irritate them.

Mrs Pelagia

On returning to the dorm, I went crazy and bought a bottle of wine. There was something to celebrate. I would find time to study for the admission exams, although I didn't know yet which field of study. I wouldn't have to worry about the rent or the cost of food. Not only that, but I would have twenty-three hours of spare time. Maybe during this time, I would learn a foreign language and possibly deepen my humanistic knowledge.

However, Alicia was not as happy as I was. When I came back, I found her drunk and babbling about her ugliness.

"In a few years, I'll graduate from college, get wrinkles, and be even uglier. If I were to graduate in economics or law, I would probably be able to afford plastic surgery. Unfortunately, I am studying cultural studies. I won't even be able to afford Botox. I will have to work as a saleswoman in my uncle's liquor store."

"I'm sure the clients will pay you compliments," I tried to make a joke.

Alicia started to cry. She looked even worse than usual, although earlier, I had doubted that was possible.

"I'm getting uglier day by day," she sobbed. "My female friends, when I encounter them, have an expression of triumph on their faces because they are prettier. Handsome men don't notice my existence. When I walk past them on the street they never look at me. They walk by like I was the air, as if I didn't exist at all. What if instead of me having walked by some sex bomb, they would probably get a heart attack from the over excitement. For a year, my hair has been falling out. In the back of my head, you can already see the gaps. My eyes are getting increasingly scooped out, and my teeth are crooked. I look like a creature from a bad fantasy novel!

"Your body is very nice," I threw in a compliment. "And your face is simply average but not ugly," I lied.

"You're lying!"

"I need to pack," I changed the subject. I started to throw my things into my backpack.

"Are you leaving?" She was surprised.

I told her briefly about the agreement with Mrs. Pelagia.

"You believed her that she would not demand sex?"

"Nothing has happened between us either, even though we have been living together," I began to explain. "And yet, everyone considers us a couple."

"Then you must be suffering immensely from this? What would Monica would say about these revelations?"

"I doubt if she would believe it," I snapped out.

"Oh yeah? Get out!" Alicia yelled, grabbing a kitchen knife.

I quickly gathered my things and retreated from the room. I had not yet seen Alicia in anger, and I had no desire to see how she behaved in such a state. I had listened earlier about her great-grandparent's rapturous characters, dueling over anything. As I ran down the dormitory stairs, I saw myself being stabbed by Ala.

I guess it will be a while before I see her again. My mood was a little spoiled by such a breakup. I thought we would sit down with wine, laugh, and talk about Mrs. Pelagia and her masks. Why couldn't Alicia accept her appearance? Everyone always liked her. At parties, she amused the company with anecdotes. Over the coffee, she spun interesting philosophical derivations, and it was sometimes difficult to follow her flow of reasoning, because it was that much sophisticated. Whenever she noticed this, she would immediately use a simple vocabulary to explain more intricate reflections. Hardly anyone commented on her ugliness. No one made fun of her appearance, and no one had to think about it except me - whom she adored, or herself.

At Mrs. Pelagia's door, I wondered about the form of apology and pardoning Alicia. Pressing the button on the intercom, I was already thinking of something else. How about Mrs. Pelagia? Will she open naked? What will happen to me then? Where will I live? No bodily close-ups were considered by me. However, I was needlessly worried. Ms. Pelagia opened the door dressed in a thick, long sweater, with an image of Santa Claus, and leggings. Her blond hair was curled in rollers.

"This is how I curl my hair from time to time when I get bored with straight hair," she began to explain.

"Then you are an original because usually women are divided into those who are proponents of either straight or curly hair."

"Yes, I know. Most often, those with naturally straight hair curl it, and those with curly hair straighten it. Please, come inside."

The apartment consisted of a living room, where bamboo light furniture reigned supreme, and on the walls hung African masks, Mrs. Pelagia's bedroom, which I preferred not to explore, and the kitchen and bathroom. What was missing was a second room for me.

"My dear, you will sleep in the lounge," Mrs. Pelagia seemed to read my mind.

"No one visits me anymore, so you can make this room a second bedroom."

"Don't you have any friends? Colleagues?" I was surprised.

"I always had friends until they met me with their husband or partner. I used to be beautiful.

They immediately were jealous, seeing the partner's attention, focused on me."

I wonder how Alicia would comment on that, I thought.

"What about men? Didn't you have friends among them?"

"First, there was my husband, who would not accept any of my male friends. He was not someone notable, despite that he seemed so promising. I would even say that he was mediocre. He graduated in philosophy but negated all the knowledge he had acquired, claiming that from thinking, people were getting mad, and that the theories he had learned were worthless. I met him in college when he was still an idealist. He talked a lot about self-discipline, shaping one's character, and working on himself. Later he ended up as a loser, sitting in front of the TV and eating up sweets because of his lost life. That's why I started cheating on him. These were not successful romances. I hoped to meet someone of value and get a divorce, but I ended up with playboys only."

"Wasn't it better to live alone?" I asked shyly.

"No. I can't be alone. I start going crazy. That's why you are here now."

An intrusive thought came to me that it was because of Mrs. Pelagia that all the men in her life were becoming losers. I did not share this reflection. One knife-threatening woman a day is enough. Besides, honesty hardly ever pays off.

"Since I've been alone, I've been going crazy in many ways. I learned to crochet and make nice sweaters, but when finished, I rip them, and from the same fibers, I make another ones. All of them are black in color. At least once a month I write denunciations of people who have in any way harmed me. Sometimes such a denunciation is more than a dozen pages long."

"Really? What do you write about there?"

"About everything, they have to hide what is illegal. I used to work for the police, so I have no problems collecting such data. Almost every Pole has some illegal programs on the computer or downloaded movies. This is punishable. When a husband cheats, I write a denunciation to his wife."

"Do you feel better about it?"

"It gives me some satisfaction, but for a short time. I have become addicted to cigarettes. I can smoke three packs a day. Every Friday, I drink whiskey alone."

"Why only on Fridays?"

"The weekend starts. Friends make appointments, and lovers go on dates, whereas I sit alone in an empty apartment, forgotten by everyone."

"If you signed your denunciations, indeed, a lot of people would remember you," I tried to joke.

"O, you won't have an easy life with such an attitude," said Mrs. Pelagia.

"Attitude is an attitude, but I would be much happier if lousy luck had left me."

I began to tell about my adventures and fate when looking for a job.

"My dear," Ms. Pelagia interrupted me, "by talking about bad luck, you put yourself in the role of a victim, a puppet tossed here and there by the twists of fate. It is not quite the most important thing that happens to us, but our reaction to the situations that arise. You can live your entire life by doing things the wrong way, blaming fate and complex and unfavorable conditions, and not trying to live actively."

"I did what I could," I answered. "After all, I was actively looking for a job after the disaster at college. I went to interviews. Is it my fault that I got shit on by a pigeon or that some woman decided to deliver a baby on the bus?"

"I think that if you approached it diplomatically, both situations could be successfully resolved. You are not yet able to properly talk to people."

"And how, for example, was I supposed to talk when I lost my voice and had a call about a call center job?"

"You lost because you let your emotions take over your body."

I guess I wasn't yet ready for the brainwashing that Mrs. Pelagia wanted to serve me. I politely apologized to her and asked if I could unpack and take a shower. I felt the daily time spent with this woman would be quite a torture.

I stuffed my things in the bamboo furniture and decided to take a long shower. In the bathroom, there was both a bathtub and a shower cabin. I was tempted to take a bath in the tub, but nowhere did I see utensils to wash it, and I didn't want to take a bath without first scrubbing the enamel surface. I recalled Mrs. Pelagia's mention of her affairs, and my thoughts revolved around the germs of STDs occupying the tub sides. So I took a shower. I usually slept in my underwear but wrapped my hips with a towel, not wanting to overexpose my body.

This is how Mrs. Pelagia saw me when I stepped into the kitchen to drink a glass of water. She gave me a lustful gaze. Her eyes glazed over, and her face covered with sweat. I felt very uncomfortable with this silent adoration.

Why do I keep getting myself into situations like this? Why, instead of Mrs. Pelagia, isn't a horny Monica sitting at the table? Now not only will I be listening to pro development gibberish, but I will also probably be molested by a fifty-year-old woman.

"Relax," said Mrs. Pelagia. "You are terribly tense. Why don't we look for some programs on the radio to listen to?"

"A broadcast?"

All I could think of were Catholic radio stations. What kind of broadcast does she want to listen to? She has brought home a young boy and will pray the rosary with him or listen to ramblings about the pure evil that is contraception, according to those running the programs?

"The full hour spent together hasn't passed yet," said Mrs. Pelagia. "Wait, I'll bring the mask."

Suddenly my stomach started to hurt. Needless to say, I was in quite a mess.

I should not have pissed Alicia off and lived with her until I found a job. After all, everyone says there are no shortcuts in life. Why didn't I think of this earlier? The offer seemed to be so simple. Probably, Mrs. Pelagia is a psychopath. Who typically makes a caller wear a mask, especially with an image of her face? Apparently, some psychopaths have a unique personal charm. Maybe that caused me to agree to live with this woman? The mask was a perfect representation of Mrs. Pelagia's face.

It was made of some kind of plastic. On the back, there was a lock. A wig was placed over the whole thing. Fortunately, it turned out to be too small for my face. Mrs. Pelagia could not get over this fact. She wanted so much to look at herself. I suggested that she look in the mirror.

She became quite indignant, and for several minutes I had to listen about the insensitivity of young people, about their stupidity and self confidence. After complaining about my generation, it was time to criticize politicians and the setup of our country.

"What kind of country is this, where plastic surgery is so expensive? Politicians only want to take advantage of working people. Once they become unfit for work and retire, they are allowed to die slowly and grow old without sufficient funds for medicines, not to mention entertainment or improving their appearance."

This was the second time I had to listen to that day about plastic surgery.

Mrs. Pelagia talked, giving prices of the various procedures and bragging about the Botox done.

"Apparently, daily gymnastics helps keep you young," I interjected.

"The audience is over," said Mrs. Pelagia.

She brought a folding bed from the basement and unfolded it in the lounge.

"If you are uncomfortable, you can always sleep with me. I have a big bed."

And so my nightmare began. Nothing was easy. I decided to stay at Mrs. Pelagia's, disregarding her eccentricities and quiet adoration of my person. Thanks to the fact that I was provided with lodging and food, I could concentrate on preparing for college. I was not going to give up on higher education just because doctor Plonski was allergic to the cheap food. On the other hand, the problem was choosing the right course of study. Studying at a previous university was out of the question, as I was given a 'wolf ticket'.

There was still a technical university in the city, but I had little talent for science subjects, so I turned down that option. All that was left for me was to move to a larger city and study there. I just didn't know what I wanted to study. Cultural studies interested me, but Alicia's speech about working in a liquor store somewhat extinguished my enthusiasm for exploring this field of knowledge.

I decided to try again to apply for psychology again. To get into these studies, it was necessary to pass a test of general knowledge and an examination of study skills. I decided to study for the exam in the library's reading room. When I was laying out books in the kitchen, Mrs. Pelagia always sat down and spun her life wisdom.

The main message of her talkative outbursts was the thesis that everyone is the blacksmith of his fate. My recent experiences were too fresh to agree with her.

To avoid these chatterboxes, I started spending time in the reading room. It was getting cold, and sitting in the park with a book was a no - go. I didn't have a lot of money for cafes, and I felt silly sitting there over one cup of coffee for several hours. The reading room was warm and dry. I usually chose a seat by the window and contemplated from time to time the nasty weather outside when I had breaks from studying.

Mrs. Pelagia called me on average eight times in one hour. I muted the phone, but I could hear the vibration of it as calls came in. I did not answer. No calls were allowed in the reading room. Besides, I had no desire to talk to her.

Usually, my day looked as follows. Mrs. Pelagia would wake me up at nine in the morning for breakfast. After breakfast I would go to the reading room for a few hours. Around two o'clock, I would return for lunch. After that, I waited patiently for our hour spent together.

Already at lunch, Mrs. Pelagia was asking why I didn't answer the phone when it rang. I explained that I spent that time in the reading room studying. Not believing me, she commented that I was probably dating some girl. I was explaining that even if I wanted to, girls go to school, college, or work at this time of the day. Mrs. Pelagia kept extending the time until our "hour." She simply wanted me to stay longer at home.

"Just a moment, my dear. I'll just watch a replay of this TV series." "Just a moment. I'll just finish reading a chapter of this book." And so on.

Finally, she graciously granted me an audience. At the same time, she smoked like a dragon, and I often choked on smoke as she smoked five cigarettes in a row.

However, I had to admit that our conversations were often fascinating. Mrs. Pelagia was well-read. She covered topics in the social sciences, and sometimes, she talked about the books she had read. She told me about various scientific theories, so it was not time wasted. After an hour spent together, I would go to the bamboo room and read books. Later there was dinner. After dinner, I would go for a walk, often in the company of Mrs. Pelagia.

She would drag me sometimes to cafes or pubs, where she bought mulled wine for us. Sometimes she was good company and in such moments I forgot about her uncompromising character. She was very fond of instructing me, and invariably she would wait for me to come out of the shower.

I missed the carefree period of my first year at university when I lived in a dormitory, and the only adverse event was when a roommate used up all of my shower gel or ate my food. Even Alicia's was better. Her adoration was more subtle than Mrs. Pelagia's. That's why when I once returned from the reading room to find Mrs. Pelagia dead, I was a little relieved.

Unwanted corpse

Mrs. Pelagia sat on a bamboo chair with a scarf wrapped tightly around her neck. Her entire face was blue and gave no signs of life. On the table in front of her stood two cups of under-drank coffee.

Could it be that someone couldn't stand the type of conversation she liked to have? It was clear that she had been murdered. By whom? Why? Am I in danger too?

I could not answer these questions. Maybe one of the victims of her denunciations wanted revenge?

My attention was caught by a whisper coming from the kitchen. I checked the source of the sound. It was the stove's gas hissing from the four open taps. Apparently, the murderer wanted to cover the traces of his crime permanently - the gas explosion would have effectively eliminated all traces of DNA from the crime scene and masked the cause of Mrs. Pelagia's death.

I turned off the taps quickly and opened the window. Not knowing how much the air was saturated with gas and whether it was safe to stay in the apartment, I left the house. The fresh air and cold wind refreshed me. I began to analyze the situation. I should have called the police and an ambulance long ago.

Why haven't I done it so far? Isn't it too late for such an activity? And what will happen to me now? I still had no contact with Alicia. I sent her a few peaceful text messages, but she did not write back. Staying with her was out of the question.

I was left in the dark. Contacts from studies had broken off, and I couldn't think of anyone who would gladly help me. I had no money to pay for a room or for food.

How about insinuating that Mrs. Pelagia was still alive? A sudden thought popped into my head. Besides me and the murderer, who could know about her death? I could count on the discretion of the murderer. Indeed he is not bragging now to some bartender about his deed.

Can I continue living in Mrs. Pelagia's apartment and pretend in front of the authorities and people that nothing happened? She was receiving her pension in a bank account. She paid her bills via the Internet. I knew all of her passwords. I knew the PIN number for her debit card. All this information was written on paper and shoved into a cookbook. I found it accidentally while looking for a recipe for a regional dish, called 'kutia'.

I had no choice. It was necessary to quietly bury Mrs. Pelagia's corpse somewhere and pretend she was still alive. No one had taken so far interest in her, so there was a chance that I would be able to live at her address for a few more months.

Just what to do with the body?

I returned to the apartment. At one time, Mrs. Pelagia had invested in a large freezer. I took out all the drawers along with the frozen content (two were dominated by garlic), emptying the interior.

The deceased was of a petite physique. She had yet to stiffen, so the bending of her body resulted in success. The corpse fit into the freezer. Mrs. Pelagia had probably never been so limber as she was after her death. I threw the frozen food drawers into the bathtub to avoid inundating my downstairs neighbors with melting water. I had never met them, and it was not the best time to make friends.

Putting the corpse in the freezer was a temporary solution.

I sat down heavily at the kitchen table. Then the phone from the freezer rang. I had forgotten to search the pockets of the deceased's pants, which was not engaging considering her condition after death. However, the phone had to be rescued before the refrigerator's cold put it to an end, like someone had done to its owner. And who is calling her? Throughout my stay with Mrs. Pelagia, I never saw her talking on the phone.

On the other hand, as soon as I left the apartment, she would start calling me. I was her living obsession, tangible and accessible. Sometimes she would stare for hours at me, with persistent, intruding sight, waiting for me to get my gaze away from the book I was reading and look at her. When sometimes I dared to do so, she would stretch her lips in a fake smile, not showing her teeth, which had yellow stains from the cigarettes she smoked.

I opened the freezer door with disgust and put my hand in the pocket of the fecal-soiled pants.

For a moment, I thought I might show respect to the deceased and wash her body, but I did not feel like seeing Mrs. Pelagia naked. I checked the last call.

The caller was Jan Metlicki. Who the hell is Jan Metlicki? Husband? A brother? Did Mrs. Pelagia's husband die, or did she divorce him? Did she keep her last name after her husband, or did she revert to her maiden name?

I lived with her for so long and could not answer these questions for myself. Mrs. Pelagia did not interest me. I acted like a cold, selfish person and took advantage of the situation, trying to have as little contact with her as possible. I did not engage in private conversations so that she would not start to despair over her loneliness. I tried to preserve my personal space unsuccessfully. Mrs.Pelagia would enter my room without knocking, usually with a slogan: "And do you know what I just remembered?" and would begin her monologue, punctuated politely by my interjections.

Sometimes she would look at me as if she wanted to kill me. Such rage and hate emanated from her face. I was afraid that she would throw me into the street. Therefore, her death brought a kind of relief. It will be what it is supposed to be, but at least the torments with this woman are over.

And couldn't it have been like before, when the whole world seemed to not remember about the two of us?

And here, some Jan Metlicki suddenly calls out a few hours after the death of this repulsive psychopath.

I checked whether Jan Metlicki is in some group of contacts. Mrs. Pelagia had everything nicely sorted, so I suspected all people were labeled correctly. Jan Metlicki was in the group of "Family" contacts.

Curious, I started looking for my name until I finally found my phone number under "Rooster."

I began to sympathize with the murderer. Who knows what kind of humiliations he had spared me.

I checked the call history and text messages on the phone.

Since the morning, Jan Metlicki had been calling her a few times. Two calls were answered and lasted one two and the other five minutes. Both were about two hours before my return. Within a few minutes, you can make an appointment for coffee.

Jan Metlicki was apparently a murderer. He called, probably intrigued by the lack of an explosion and no media coverage of the story, how such a beautiful tenement in the town center had gone down in history because of the carelessness, or suicide attempt, of a retired woman.

What would be his next step? The vision of living alone on the premises of the deceased woman was tempting, provided that no one denounced me that the woman was dead. Currently, after my actions, I could be profiled as the prime suspect.

Just in case, I took a picture of Mrs. Pelagia's phone screen, which showed calls from Jan Metlicki. The data could soon disappear, and they were the only evidence that someone else might have seen her before she died.

I sat at the kitchen table again and analyzed the situation. Theoretically, I could have lived in the deceased's apartment for several decades. I was even authorized by her to receive mail at the Post Office. Mrs. Pelagia did not keep in touch with anyone; no one ever asked about her, no one knocked on the door, and no one called. Her solitude was almost caricatured.

The murderer remained. Currently, about the death of my sponsor, only he and I knew, unless more people were involved in the whole thing. No one else should find out about this death.

Nevertheless, I felt an irresistible urge to share this problem with someone. I was far too young for such experiences. I should now be drinking beer with students and talking over lecturers or making grandiose plans that would contribute to new ideologies, completely changing the world for the better. In reality, I was sitting beside a corpse, separated from them only by the refrigerator door. And I was financially dependent on the dead woman.

I decided to contact Alicia. If only she didn't think about her appearance, she had a common-sense approach to most things. Could she give me some advice?

It would be appropriate to get rid of the corpse, but I had yet to learn how to do it at the moment.

Surprisingly, Alicia answered the phone after just the second beep.

"Hi, gigolo!" She shouted into the receiver. "What position did you propose to the old lady today? Doesn't her spine protest?"

Like most people, I always suspected that my phone calls were being overheard. I thought it was just my paranoia, but it turned out to be shared by most of my peers.

Often, my colleagues would stop the conversation mid-sentence, saying it couldn't be told over the phone. Recently, however, I have shed these fears.

Perhaps because of the large amount of knowledge I had absorbed, I felt small and uninteresting. Therefore, I immediately fired back:

"Ala, she can't have sex because she's stiff."

"Age does its own thing. She certainly won't be as fit as Monica."

"Ala, she's dead!"

"She couldn't stand the missionary position anymore?"

"I put the corpse in the refrigerator. Someone killed her. Don't you know how to get rid of the body?"

"Why are you calling me with this? I'm from an orphanage, not from a family of criminals."

"You have an uncle who runs a liquor store. He certainly has access to the mafia. So maybe you know some helpful stories."

"I made this uncle up. I don't know anyone from my family."

"What do you mean you made it up? After all, you never lie!"

"What makes you so sure? If I am ugly, I must supposedly have a crystal character? And I love the whole world plus I have an interesting personality, because, after all, it is not the appearance that counts, but the character's qualities? Or my inside is ugly too. I may have an evil character and don't like people. Maybe I am a sociopath?"

"That last one would be handy right now," I muttered. "We need to get rid of the corpse."

"After all, it's your problem. Call Monica! And why are you talking about it on the phone?"

"No one overhears us; we are ordinary students."

"So what, if I'm ugly, does that mean no one can eavesdrop?"

"Ala, please stop talking about your ugliness already. Haven't you noticed that you are also fat?"

"What?"

Having grabbed Alicia's attention for a while, I began to refer to recent events. Ala interrupted me every now and then, mocking me. I felt uncomfortable. I did not know what to say for the old Alicia to return. Cheerful, treating everything with enthusiasm, gushing with optimism. And in addition, I felt that the culprit of her awful transformation into a complaining grandmother was myself. I was the one who rejected her affection and destroyed her self-confidence.

"Didn't you watch the movies? The body gets buried somewhere in the deep forest." I was interrupted from these thoughts by Alicia.

"I don't have a car to haul her away."

'Then rent one. Or take the bus."

The vision of thawing a frozen body in the bus's cargo hold was not appealing. The idea of renting a car was more sensible. Just where to transport the body? Although the city was surrounded by forest, it grew on rocky hills, and the trees were dwarfed. How would I dig a hole in the ground like this? I could sink the body in a nearby river, attaching a ballast so it would not float away. The second option was less certain.

The body could have floated out and been identified. My brain could not come up with a sensible solution. Should I live with the corpse in the refrigerator for the next few years?

I decided to take a step towards getting rid of the corpse and stock up on a spade.   A memorable supermarket on the outskirts of the town was open until midnight. My initial thought was to buy the spade already after renting the car, as I wanted to have a few people seeing me with this tool.

However, the fear that someone would then check the trunk and find the body of Mrs. Pelagia made me decide to go and get the tool without the company of the corpse.

This time no one sickened me, but bad luck did not let go. Pumped up with adrenaline, I walked through a small pedestrian crossing near the supermarket at a red light, and suddenly I heard:

"You wait there."

A policeman stood mingled with a group of people, meekly waiting for the light to change, even though no car was passing. Typically I would have run away, but I was afraid to mess with the police in the current situation.

So I waited politely, terrified as I had never been in my life. After the lights changed, a policeman approached me and pulled out a block of fine tickets.

"Where are we going in such a hurry?" He asked.

"It was cold, and no cars drove through, so..." I began to explain.

"ID, please."

I pulled out the document and handed it to the policeman, who checked the address and asked:

"Why so far from home? Are we studying here?"

"No, I'm looking for a job."

"And what are you using the spade for at this time of year? We may be growing something in the greenhouse."

"Certainly not; what are you accusing me of!"

"What am I accusing you of? After all, you can grow some tomatoes. And what did you think of?"

I felt pressure in my throat, a well-known sign that I was losing my voice. Always at the most critical moments, this must have happened to me. My larynx tightened, and only a mouse-like squeak could be heard.

At the same time, I wondered how to get out of the current situation. How to explain the damn spade? And what to do with the policeman's suspicion about the illegal cultivation of marijuana? What address to give?

Suddenly I remembered the various strange offers of volunteering, where, for example, you had to pay a fat subsidy to sit somewhere in the African wilderness and count eggs on a farm.

I decided to lie.

"You see, this spade is for volunteering," I squeaked. "I found an ad for helping pensioners on allotments, and apparently, volunteering is welcome on a resume when applying for better corporate jobs."

"Right? And who organizes this volunteering?" Asked the policeman, sniffing me indiscreetly.

"Brother Edgar," I answered, glancing at the business card taken out with the document.

"Is it after this brother that you have such a soft voice?" The policeman apparently was not fond of the clergy. "Go to the army, and stop lick monks' asses!" He yelled.

Several people passing by stopped, airing a scandal. There were no games in the city, so people were thirsty for entertainment, even an argument. And how nice it is to watch when someone is in trouble, and we avoid it.

"After all, there is no longer an obligation to do military service." I said.

"Then shovel! Dig ditches!"

"I just bought a spade."

"Are you going to dig gardens for a priest?"

"Officer, you can't do that," interrupted an onlooker with a mustache. "You have to be tolerant these days. Especially in this position."

The policeman wheezed with anger and began to write me a fine.

I meekly accepted the fine and walked up to the tram, trying not to walk too fast so as not to arouse another suspicion.

At home, I pushed the spade deep into the bamboo closet, and then I realized that I had left my ID card in the hands of a policeman, and, out of sensitivity, I did not take the document back.

The only document left proving my identity was my driver's license. More was needed to rent a car. Well, I simply needed a partner for this crime, and here I suddenly realized that I was as lonely as a finger in this city.

After flunking out of college, I felt ashamed to hang out with my classmates. They supposedly knew I was in town, but no one ever called to ask me out for a beer, invite me to a party, or meet for the proverbial coffee.

It was as if I had ceased to exist after being expelled from college.

However, my relationships with other students were loose; even if I had some contact with them, I would probably be afraid to ask for help. I could trust only Alicia.

Was it right to put her in trouble with the law?

It was enough that she was an ugly student. I wanted to make her an ugly prisoner. I felt bad. In the freezer reigned the corpses, and I had no income to leave the apartment and start living independently. No one cared about me except my parents, but I couldn't tell them anything. I decided to wait out the situation. It could not affect the sudden appearance of the proper grounds on the nearby hills to bury the body, but I hoped that I would come up with some brilliant idea and the situation would end happily.

Then came this letter from the lawyer.

Chance

The letter terrified me. It was addressed to Mrs. Pelagia Metlicka, and the District Court was listed as the sender.

I quickly picked the rest of the letters out of the mailbox - I did it late at night so as not to run into neighbors - and rushed to the apartment. I could feel the blood pulsing in my brain as I opened the letter and I feared I would have a stroke before I read the content.

The court's interest in the deceased's person was not helpful in the current situation. I would have been most happy with a letter in which an anonymous helper would tell me the time and day to collect the corpse of my sponsor to annihilate them in some way known only to anonymous helpers. The anonymous helper could not be a criminal, as he later could blackmail me. It was to be a so-called cleaner after the dirty work. I have been dreaming about him for the past week. One of the dreams was so vivid that I ran to the freezer to check if the deceased was still there.

Until then, the bills had only been coming. The letter from the court was a surprise. It was recommended in its content that Mrs. Pelagia contacted the law office of Switalski & Jarosz.

There were no details of the case, only the phone number, office hours, address, and reference number.

I sat at the kitchen table, which lately, instead of tasty food, I had begun to associate with frustrating meditations. I sat at it for quite a while, trying to find a solution to get rid of the corpse. This time, too, I didn't come up with anything promising a happy ending to the case.

I tried to think calmly and logically. Usually, there is some time to comply with the court's decision. One can write appeals and various delaying letters. And the received letter was not any final decision, just a request to go to the legal office and contact its staff. If Mrs. Pelagia doesn't respond, which she couldn't, another letter will probably arrive after a while.

Knowing the slowness of any such institutions, it would take about a month before the following document was delivered. After a month, I could write back on behalf of Mrs. Pelagia, which she should not be too offended about, noting that she could not pay a visit due to poor health or planned travel.

Worse, if one wanted to call her as a witness, she probably wouldn't be able to go anywhere, but it would have been written right away if that was the issue.

So I would then have another two weeks. A month and a half total. By then, I would have looked for a job and moved out of the apartment, cleaning it of my DNA with dozens of cleaning specs unless I found a better way to remove the traces of my presence.

I mechanically reviewed the rest of the mail. There were bills and some health magazines that Mrs. Pelagia ordered as if wanting to rehabilitate with this gesture her smoking. One of the letters probably came from some office, as the addressee's data was printed on the sticker. There were no details of the sender.

This puzzled me. Mrs. Pelagia's life was more complex, even though it gave the impression of a barren, dull existence punctuated by sudden spurts and preoccupation with personal development.

Inside the envelope was a letter with words cut from newspapers.

I felt uncomfortable. The contents of the letter were as follows:

"Dear Madam!

Has your neck stopped hurting yet? Since our last meeting, a few days have passed. Have you analyzed my proposal? I'm counting on another session; I'll buy coffee."

Under the note, there was zero signature. I was a bit frozen by this letter. It was clear that it came from a murderer. At first, I was happy.

Here I had proof that I was not the one who contributed to the woman's death. However, after thinking things over, I concluded that this was insufficient evidence. The list should include only my fingerprints. I could have written and sent the letter myself. Some clues could have been a printed sticker. Apparently, investigators have ways to verify that the prints came from a particular machine. Would they want to check? I doubted it.

I guessed that the letter was written by Jan Metlicki. Apparently, he was concerned about the lack of any information about the death of Mrs. Pelagia. It was as if nothing had happened. No gas explosions, announcements about the end, or articles about the ongoing investigation. There were no obituaries, no funeral. I wondered about the reason for sending the letter and its content. Could it be that the murderer actually wanted a meeting?

What was his motive? Maybe he wants to intimidate me? I must admit that he succeeded in doing so. Just what could he get out of Mrs. Pelagia's death? Perhaps he wanted to inherit her apartment?

However, he would not have turned off the gas after all. Maybe the deceased woman knew too much, and now the murderer suspects I have this troublesome knowledge?

One thing was clear. I had to find a job and move out as soon as possible. I stuck to this mantra as if created by some guru. In this case, that guru was social norms, one of which was that money is gained by working. I decided to look for a job directly, rather than through the Internet. I printed out about a hundred copies of my resume and hit the town in the morning, wanting to distribute the document to as many employers as possible.

And then something strange happened. In one of the restaurants, the waitress to whom I handed my resume said they were just looking for someone for several months. She took the summary to the manager.

He appeared after a few minutes, took a look at me, and said:

"I won't start mugging you with questions. This job is certainly not the dream of a man your age unless you are gay. You present yourself well. I will accept you for a week and see if you're suitable. You start tomorrow."

I was in shock. Where's my bad luck? What's going on? I got the job!

I immediately called Alicia. I hadn't heard from her since the last phone call when I asked for an idea to get rid of the corpse. I was angry and disappointed that she didn't want to help. After some time, I realized that such help goes beyond the framework of friendship and, in a court of law, comes under the heading of complicity in a crime or complicity in concealing a crime.

I admitted my selfishness, but somehow I couldn't think positively about her again. I felt betrayed.

More than a year of acquaintance and everything spoiled by Alicia's complexes. She left me alone with my problems.

I should understand this. I was finally of legal age, and, despite my young age, I should accept responsibility for my actions and their consequences. Instead of going to the funeral, it was necessary to attend the exam. Instead of covering up the university doctor's affair, one should have talked about it. Instead of getting wrapped up in sponsorship with Mrs. Pelagia, one had to wait and look for a regular job. Well, with Alicia, it was necessary to get around more diplomatically. All these considerations became insignificant upon the news of getting a job. I felt such incredible joy and relief that I had to share it with someone.

Alicia answered the phone after the first ring.

"Just quickly, because I just entered the class," I heard her voice.

I was in public, so I couldn't discuss my adventures with corpses and strange correspondence. I focused on my new job.

"Buy black shirts; that's what the staff wears there," Alicia advised.

"How do you know?"

"We often go there after classes because the prices are slightly higher than a sandwich bar."

These student visits explained the early opening hours of the restaurant. I felt uneasy. I will have to face my colleagues as a serving waiter. And what will I answer to questions about what has been happening to me and what I have been doing for the past months? Did Alicia remain discreet?

The first day of work was a gehenna. I was confused by the numbers of the tables, which were not written down anywhere, so orders often landed on the wrong tables. I made enemies out of all the older ladies who were regular customers.

Unfortunately, they tried to flirt with me, and I, nervous in my new role, would only mumble something.

For example, after placing an order, one of these ladies told me a compliment.

"What an elegant shirt you have! And how nicely it wraps around biceps!"

"When I was younger, they were bigger. With age, they fade somewhere," I replied.

A blush bloomed on the old lady's cheeks. Only then I realized that mentioning age in certain situations is not tactful. I didn't get any tips either. Sometimes someone said that the change was unnecessary, but they were usually pennies to compensate. For example, there was 15.99 zloty to pay, and someone in a strained voice said, giving 16 zlotys: "You don't need to give me the change."

Other employees carried several plates at once, placing them on their forearms. I was dashing with the tray several times to the same table. Traffic was heavy.

The job consisted of approaching new guests, picking up the order, then bringing the dishes, and, after some time, making sure the customers paid. I liked it when customers paid by card because there was no need to give change. At dispensing, I sometimes got confused out of anticipation. Eventually I started carrying a calculator and subtracted money due from the received amount to see a sum of change.

This did not look very professional, and customers suspiciously recalculated the money received. During my work, I noticed that I was adored by female customers. These women would not pay attention to me if I walked past them down the street. Here, they worshiped me. I felt lustful glances on my buttocks. As I approached them, the giggles of the younger female customers pestered me. I was most annoyed when female clients were looking at me, even though they were in the company of men.

I could understand some of these ladies. Their partners were significantly obese, with their bellies not fitting under the table, so they often sat half a meter away from the table, separated from it by their fatty tissue. Added to this were greasy hair and the smell of sweat. Sometimes some men were very attractive, but even that did not stop their women from giving me attention.

After a week, I noticed that different groups of customers were coming at other times. First thing in the morning, the old ladies were coming in. Later, students came in between classes, and from late afternoon into the evening - couples.

After the first few days of work, most of the old ladies had already managed to get offended by me, and now serving them was quite an unpleasant task. Nothing hurts more than injured pride. Although I tried to rebuild trust, the grandmothers were not fooled by false compliments and courtesies.

They grumbled at the slow service, even though I could not be accused of that. They complained about the weather and the prices on the menu. However, they did not grab knives like offended Alicia, so I was used to their grumpiness.

The students mistreated me. In their eyes, I came off as a bumbling loser who is so stupid that he can't afford a better job. I couldn't have the future ahead of me that they dreamed of. They probably thought I had no greater ambitions than working in this restaurant for the next thirty years.

This irritated me, and I often felt like speaking in some scientific jargon, but there was never an opportunity to do so because it would have been rude to interfere in their conversations. The only chance to shine with intelligence was when they placed orders and when they were paying. At that time, however, I could only think of a gluten-free diet and fatalism, so I preferred to keep quiet.

I also experienced a particular torment when couples came together in the evenings. The restaurant could have had a better reputation. It was something a little better than a snack bar. Therefore, the women invited here for dinner by their partners had sour faces. Right next door were two expensive restaurants and led in that direction, ladies usually thought that this was where they would be dining.

When they entered my eatery, their faces showed a fresh expression of disappointment. They pretended to be pleasant and content with life for the rest of the evening. At the same time, ostentatiously they coquetted all the waiters as if making it clear that they don't mind the choice of venue because, after all, they are modest, and the company of a partner makes up for any inconveniences. Still, nevertheless, other men in this world may one day lead them to neighboring establishments.

Of course, I did not get any tips, so they were unlikely to count on me to suddenly get rich, fall in love with them, and show them around in the evenings at all expensive restaurants.

Most of the men pretended to be calm and, in return, winked eyes at the waitresses. However, all the female staff was unearthly ugly here. I don't know on what terms and who decided on their recruitment, but they definitely could not be a competition for female customers. Even Alice would have gained in their company.

The time finally came when she showed up at my place with her "pack." These were a few people with the highest grade points. Apparently, Alicia was hoping that she would forget about me in the circle of intelligent and well-read people, as she had not mated with anyone before. Her companions and comrades - of course, Monica was not there - did not greet me when I approached.

"Hey, how are you guys doing?" I asked, somewhat puzzled.

"You are exploring the secrets of pork, and we are still exploring the complexities of culture," said Jack.

The others were nicer, but only a little. They began to ask how was work, as if they were descending to my level for a moment, only to soon restart the discussion about Freud or Goffman. When ordering, nothing interesting came to mind, so I said that probably everything contained gluten.

"Dude, you'll be out of here fast if you talk like that!" Stated Mark.

"Oh, fast, even faster than he thinks!" A female voice reached me from behind.

I turned around. The woman looked familiar, but I could not associate where I knew her from.

"Well darling, don't you recognize me?"

The past refused to forget me. It was Aneta, the woman supposed to pay me for the chat, while she preferred to crave for sex. Now she is sure to say something about the situation and ridicule me in the eyes of my friends. The gossip about my stupidity will be joined by rumors of prostitution.

I cared about my good reputation. Maybe I was driven by vanity, but I wanted to be admired and envied for my success, imaginary for now.

"I apologize very much, but I cannot have private conversations at work," I replied in the most congenial tone of voice so as not to enrage the woman.

"With me, you can, dear. I am the owner of the premises. When you finish taking the order, report to me in the office. I feel like having a very deep conversation!"

"Is this the lady from the gigolo ad? Do you have fresh underwear? I can lend you my panties. I just bought a few pairs." Said Alicia after Aneta left. "This lady probably won't disdain your ass, even if it was dressed in women's underwear."

"I don't know what you're talking about!" I gasped.

I lost my voice again.

"Listen, man, we came to eat something, and it's already been ten minutes since we tried to place an order with you. We have little interest in whether you have fresh panties. We prefer fresh food and quickly because we have another lecture soon," replied Jack.

I took the order from them quickly. Carrying it to the kitchen, I bumped into the manager.

"The owner came in and wanted to talk to you. She's a cool woman, you tell her a few compliments and you don't have to worry about anything," he said.

Aneta was already used to flattery in this place.

"What nice thing will you say to me?" She initiated the conversation when I entered the office.

I looked at her closely, wanting to come up with a compliment. A nice word about her hairstyle was out - she still had ten-centimeter roots. Her complexion was yellow and with cracked capillaries. Eyes were bloodshot and puffy. Under the tight sweater, folds of fat stood out.

"It seems you have a pleasant personality," I said uncertainly.

"It was for sure very evident when I chased you naked. I certainly did it in a very nice and endearing way!" Replied Aneta gruffly.

"I just wasn't ready for any close-up," I mumbled.

"I can give you some time, but you must be mine. I have always had a weakness for brunettes with green eyes."

'There are contact lenses."

"Will you be nice to me or not? Everyday we get a dozen resumes for jobs."

"I won't be nice."

I'll have to spend a bit more with Pelagia in the freezer, but I've had enough humiliation from pushy females.

I left the office, picked up my things, and headed toward the exit. Behind me, I heard the hurried tapping of heels. Convinced that it was Aneta, I growled over my shoulder:

"Fuck off, fat cow."

"That's how you greet me?"

It was Monica's voice. She was just stomping out of the restroom as a soiled ribbon of toilet paper was attached to her shoe.

"He has a bossy mistress. You don't stand a chance," giggled Jack from his table.

"I will despair for a long time because of this," Monica replied to him, to the delight of my former colleagues.

Only Alicia did not laugh. She looked at me with a severe gaze. I felt regret that gone were the days when she would come up and talk to me in such a situation. I was left alone with my problems.

I did not explain to Monica that my words were directed at someone else. It was even a good thing from the fact of this slight misunderstanding.

At least I was able to get out of this horrible situation with remains of pride. I hastily put on my jacket and went outside the premises. I had not yet managed to close the door when I felt the familiar pang. I was being shit on again by a pigeon.

Depression

The days came when my only company was frozen Pelagia. After leaving the restaurant, I became depressed and lost the will to fight. I holed up in Pelagia's apartment and only went out to get groceries. I had to do my shopping quite often, as the freezer was occupied by my sponsor. I also had an unpleasant conversation with my parents over the phone. They received my ID card in the mail.

A bailiff also knocked on their door, regarding arrears in student loan payments. Previously, letters had come, but my parents wouldn't open them, waiting for me to arrive. The bank attempted to contact me for several months, after which it referred the case to the collection department.

Thus, my parents found out that I was not studying.

"You were so smart... What happened?" Cried my mother into the phone receiver. "Are you taking drugs?"

"This is a temporary situation. Since October I will study again."

"Come back home! Your father will get you a job in the uncle Henrik's food processing factory!"

"Mom, I work in the library now," I lied. "I can read books at work and study for exams, because before noon only a few people come."

"Kid, I know when you are lying," I heard the pained voice of my mother. "Come back!"

"I have to go, some reader came," I replied and switched off the phone.

The conversation motivated me to pull myself together.

It was necessary to pay off the loan. Parents can not afford such an expense, and it was not right for them to lose their belongings after being seized by the bailiff, because of my silly adventures.

That still left a problem of Uncle Henrik, who was the loan's guarantor. He had the money to pay off the debt, but I would forever remain the family loser, if I allowed him to pay back the loan.

I texted my mother that I would be repaying the debt and to come to an agreement with the bank on what amount per month I should transfer. Pelagia's pension allowed her to pay off the debt. Only how long would I be able to use this benefit?

I was in the restroom when I heard again the sound of an incoming call. I didn't manage to answer it. It was Alicia. I quickly called back.

"Hey gigolo, I won a triple jackpot and I can afford to buy you a coffee," she mumbled.

She was obviously drunk, even though it was only eleven in the morning. I didn't want to hang out with her in such a state at the pub. She could make a row and talk too much about Pelagia.

"Come over to my place, I have your favorite chocolate," I replied.

"After all, I do not eat chocolate."

"What do you mean, there was always coffee flavored one in the refrigerator."

"You don't know anything about women, even the ugly ones," said Alicia. "I kept it so as not to eat sweets. As I knew it was at hand, I did not think about them so much."

"How about me? Do you also want to meet to forget my humble person?"

"No... I l... I like you."

I became uncomfortable and grateful that she did not finish that unfortunate expression. I forced her to order a cab. I unhurriedly went downstairs, the cab was due to arrive in a few minutes.

Alicia was dressed in a long black coat. One could not see any skirt, just her shapely legs, in tights with a sexy pattern and in long stilettos. Getting out of the car, she swayed slightly on them, but quickly regained her balance.

Meanwhile, I turned pale, worrying whether under her coat she has any clothes on. Maybe she's naked and will discard the coat in the apartment? Why are all the women molesting me lately?

I invited her into the kitchen. The living room where I slept, after a period of my depression, still looked neglected, so I couldn't show it to her. On the furniture were piled dirty clothes, on the floor lying boxes of pizza, which I sometimes ordered when I ran out of food in the fridge and didn't want to go to the store.

Alice politely sat down in the kitchen. The silence began. She did not take off her coat, for which I was grateful.

"How are you doing with your studies?" I asked. "What are you covering now in your philosophy classes?"

"We are redoing those ... That's a difficult word, I think I'm too drunk to say it.... I drank two and a half bottles of wine... For courage... I wanted to see you..."

"I'm happy with your decision. I haven't seen you for a long time."

"And I want to see your hubby."

"Here you go," I opened the freezer door, without getting into the explanation that nothing happened between me and Pelagia.

"Nice... Will you leave me alone for a while?"

"What do you want to do!" I freaked out. Alicia has long ago lost so-called common sense and has become a rather unpredictable individual. However, I left the kitchen.

"You can come in," I heard after a while, at which point I imagined Alicia slitting her wrists or pulling the hair out of the head of a corpse. Concerned about what awaited me, I entered the kitchen.

Sitting at the table was Pelagia, in a little black dress.

"Do you like me now?" She asked in Alice's voice.

"What do you mean... What..."

"Mask, stupid!"

Well, yes. Pelagia's face mask. How could I have forgotten about it? Now that I knew where Pelagia's head had come from on Alicia's body, I could see the places by the mouth and eyes, where the mask ended and Alicia's face began.

"The connections can be covered up," said my friend, as if guessing my thoughts.

"Awesome! You can go out with me like this to...."

"Then without a mask I can no longer go out anywhere with you?" She interrupted me in mid-sentence. "I think I wasted my time coming here."

She pulled off the mask and reached for her coat.

"You don't understand anything!" I shouted. "You can pretend to be Pelagia! You will save my ass!"

"How many times is it? Ah! I would have forgotten to share with you gossip. Magda from our group is pregnant, and Monica is dating some lawyer. Your favorite has chosen a winner."

It made me sad. Everyone, including my parents, considered me a loser. Someone who had already lost his life and whose only vocation is putting cucumbers and salads into jars in my uncle's processing plant. I was the only one who believed that this was a temporary situation.

That in a few months I will pass for a good college in a better city, that I will finish some major field of study that holds a bright future, that I'll open my own business, and that I'll be able to afford to travel a few months per year.

I didn't yet know what I would study or what my company would be. I was just sure I'll rise above the average. Or maybe my dreams and goals were right for the average mind? Based on consuming goods and collecting experiences? Everyone dreams of a super profession that will give them lots of money. Everyone dreams of traveling, well, maybe with the exception of my former restaurant manager, who has traveled the farthest twenty kilometers from his place of birth.

Maybe my dreams and goals should be less trivial? Maybe I should invent a new political system? Get involved in improving the world?

"What's got you so bogged down," Alicia interrupted my contemplation. "Don't worry, she will quickly get bored and be free. To seduce a doctor of medicine."

"Ala, I don't think about her at all lately. I've been thinking more about you than about Monica. I feel sorry for our friendship."

"You say that because you need me to pretend to be that old grandmother."

"Yes, you are needed by me. As a friend."

Alicia puffed out her lips and looked at me, trying to open wide eyes. I don't know if I passed the test of sincerity, because she suddenly rolled her eyes, put her head on the table and started snoring.

I had never heard her snore before. Where did it suddenly come from? Or maybe I always fell asleep before her and that's why I didn't hear anything? It made me uncomfortable. Will I never come across a normal woman?

Alicia's hair had fallen down, covering her face. Now one could see quite an attractive girl. Shapely shoulders, firm bust, slender waist, shapely legs.... However, I was no longer deceived, like the first time I saw her. There, under that hair, lurks her face, with which, without any makeup, she could get a zombie role in any, even the most ambitious film production. And that hair, which looked like she teased it every half an hour. Maybe, if she had tied them up, she would have looked better?

It was getting late. It was my time to check the mail. I listened to Alicia's snoring to see if it was fake. I didn't believe anyone anymore. Maybe she's faking it, and when I leave, she'll throw the frozen Pelagia out the window as revenge.

It seemed to me that Ala was actually asleep, so I quietly left the apartment and went to get the letters. Without checking them, I took the whole bundle and rushed to the apartment. The girl was still asleep.

One of the letters was sent by the office of Switalski & Jarosz. They informed that they had important information to pass on about Anna Metlicka's inheritance. They asked to appear as soon as possible at their law office.

I felt myself sweating. Could it be that inheritance was the cause of Pelagia's death? If so, what amount was it that Jan Metlicki decided to commit murder? And what should I do with this revelation? If they don't see Pelagia in the office, they will think that something is not right. In theory she could ignore the letter from the court, but not the news of the inheritance.

The information probably caused people immediately after receiving it to show up at the legal office, never mind the fact that they were wearing slippers and without makeup. The word "inheritance" has great power. It is possible that it does not please people who lost a loved one.

Whether Anna Metlicka could have been someone close to her? Would Pelagia have gone to the lawyers in mourning, or dressed in colorful clothes, as if going to a carnival ball? I tore my eyes away from the letter and looked confusedly around the kitchen. My gaze hung on Alicia's calf. She was dressed in black. She could go in the morning to the office, after practicing a few points, but how to encourage her to do so? If she were a drug addict, the case would be clear.

I would offer her a few drugs, after completing the task, and we would part ways in agreement. She would call every few days, asking if I needed a Pelagia double. However, Alicia had no known addictions. She didn't even drink coffee or tea.

Apparently, she was supposed to look better because of it. I don't know how she could look worse. Maybe it will happen in a dozen or so years, when her cheeks sag and furrows emerge on her forehead. And yet, despite her ugliness, I felt moved as I watched her sleeping. So many memories connected me with this girl. Hundreds of cafe sittings in between classes.

Long disputes about the systems that govern the world, about our individuality and resistance to top-down programming.

Not contaminated by going to a hated job, not overwhelmed by the daily chores, with disdain, we discussed the flaws of the typical, gray man, who goes to work, then eats in front of the TV or drinks vodka. We considered ourselves different, better, "enlightened." With us, no one will be able to do this trick, we won't give in to everyday life.

And let's take my example. Barely closed the doors of the university in front of me, the first thing I did was to start looking for a job. And I was not choosy about job positions. I often applied for inferior positions that would not satisfy the average citizen, whom we made fun of so much. Once I even sent in an application for the position of toilet administrator in the men's restrooms at railway station. And I thought it was not derogatory to my dignity, that after work I would find time to study.

So the work was indifferent, and suddenly the money started to count. It was so nice to theorize when my parents deposited part of the money into my account, and the rest of the expenses were covered by a student loan. In a clash with reality, only stoicism was a useful philosophy, promising happiness even in the position of a toilet worker. And how much time does such a worker have to read!

I ended up as a keeper. I was not able, despite my intelligence, to find even the worst job.

It dented my self-confidence. I looked at the sleeping girl now and was reminded of all our conversations, from before my "fall." What a talker I was back then. With every scientific text I read I was getting more and more brilliant. And now?

Our ideas and beliefs proved to be inadequate to life's situations. Alicia was not yet aware of this. Sometimes she mumbled something about the lack of prospects after this field of study, but she immediately added that after defending her master's thesis, she would pass exams for a doctorate. Same as wanted to do the majority of people in the year. Everyone felt smart enough.

Alicia did not yet know that in order to defend her PhD, she would have to take on additional work, if only as a hotel cleaner, because not everyone gets a stipend for a PhD. And that after defending her doctorate in cultural studies, and without help with getting a job through the 'network', she would be at the same point as after defending her master's degree, only that a few years older.

How great will her bitterness be when she will "realize" this? How deep will the furrows appear on her face when she takes a job that involves, for example, writing documents at the City Hall, or stamping papers at the job center?

I took out a blanket from Pelagia's closet and covered the sleeping girl.

"Just a few more minutes," she mumbled.

I wondered what to do. To leave her in the kitchen, in the company of the frozen Pelagia, or wake her up? Or maybe move to the bedroom?

The heavy snoring prompted me to abandon any violent moves. I left Alice in the kitchen and I went to sleep in my living room.

After Pelagia died I was able to move to the bedroom, but the idea of sleeping in the bed, where the body of this abusive woman was lying, was horrible.

I continued to sleep on an uncomfortable guest bed, which sometimes with a loud clatter folded in half, because the corresponding lock was loosened.

I could not fall asleep. I wondered how to get Alicia to cooperate. Maybe offer her half of the inheritance, suggesting that it would be enough for her to get a decent plastic surgery?

And if she does the surgery, will she count on my romances and be disappointed? Will she remain discreet? And what is inheritance exactly consisting of?

An apartment? Furniture? The savings of some stingy old lady, who has been eating bread with margarine all her life, just to accumulate a sum of money in a sock? My thoughts returned to Alice and the imaginary plastic surgery. What would such a surgeon have to do? Perhaps it would be enough if the zombie-like bruises from under her eyes were removed, and eyes themselves were less exfoliated? Some kind of nose correction?

I thought of my friend with compassion. Any corrections seemed to have little effect. But after all, there are plenty of so-called ugly people who found partners and live in happy relationships.

Maybe I should find Alicia a partner? Or maybe I should become her partner myself?

I tried to imagine us in an intimate situation.

I began to wonder what Alicia's face looked like at the moment of orgasm, and the longer I tried to imagine it, the greater was the desire to match my friend with someone.

I turned on the bedside lamp and searched for a popular dating site. I found a reasonably tolerable picture of Ala. It wasn't perfect. Instead of a pink dress that would have attracted admirers, she was wearing combat pants and sneakers, but her face looked better than it did in reality. I thought for a long time about a nickname and finally I chose "Alice_in_the_wonderland."

I left filling in the description boxes for later. Well, how should I describe her? Will anyone be interested in intelligence? Most people are attracted to photographs. Certainly a brilliant text would have scored her points, but at this time I was unable to produce anything convincing.

I wrote down details like height and weight, improvising slightly, since these data were unknown to me. I thought for a long time about how to determine her eye color. In the end, I typed in brown, feeling that I would face a storm for this in the future.

I   saved   the   changes   and
"Alice_in_the_wonderland" began to exist.

Plans

In the morning a brilliant idea came to my mind. Someone a few years ago, or maybe even earlier, invented the telephone. After all, Pelagia could call a lawyer instead of bothering to go in person. Admittedly, the phrase "inheritance" should awaken stronger emotions and actions in her than simply reaching for the phone, but it was worth trying.

For example, "Pelagia" could have concluded that her aunt had nothing valuable, or at least nothing known to her. It was like trying to shoot with a secured gun, but I couldn't think of something better.

The mask was not reliable. From a distance of a few meters it could give me heart palpitations, as it did yesterday, but it would not deceive someone from a distance of a several inches, which is the "handshake" distance.

What if it was generally known that the aunt was rich?

Although I found no information about her on the Internet, she was probably an older person with little or no activity on social media.

Another issue - would the lawyer say anything specific over the phone? I had a reference number and knew Pelagia's identification numbers, but such matters usually required an in-person appearance at the office, or an institution.

Next matter - the inheritance must have been powerful, if someone was able to kill for it. Yet there are known situations when someone kills for a few zlotys.

I began to listen to the sounds from the kitchen. Is Alicia still there? She can't escape me, monkey.

I got up and - remembering Pelagia's gaze - I dressed carefully.

Alicia was sitting at Pelagia's laptop. Next to her was an open cookbook with passwords... just as I had left it there.

"'Are you also a devotee of kutia?" Alicia asked mockingly. "Guess what I bought myself. I also must have some fun out of this gig."

"Ala!" I shouted. "I still haven't paid her bills this month."

"Look!" She turned the laptop in my direction.

The screen showed a blonde wig.

"It's always better than coloring," I began diplomatically.

How long had Alicia been shopping? Knowing her abilities in this area, I could be sure that if she sat on the computer for more than half an hour, the entire pension of the former police woman would have gone to buy books. The wig didn't match that. What gave me faint hope that the worst was yet to come.

"I also bought green lenses."

"Oh."

"Aren't you happy?"

"You really don't look that bad," I said. "Maybe if you got rid of those bags under your eyes..." I decided to be sincere a bit.

"These are the bruises of an intellectual," Ala replied with superiority. "Mediocrities prefer to sleep for a dozen hours at a time, while I sleep for four."

I really wanted to interrupt her and tell that the bags did not appear there yesterday, but she has had them since I have known her. And in the dormitory when I lived with her she slept from eight to ten hours.

"It's called "Elementary School Action"," Alicia continued.

"What did you get involved in again? Are you walking children across the street?"

"You don't understand anything. In elementary school I really studied and it gave results. Later, I just counted on short-term memory. And now I have decided to spend more time on studying. I also want to study psychology. We will go to college together."

"Sooner you will visit me in the prison," I sighed.

"I ordered an express delivery. I'll do it for you."

"So, what do you mean?"

"I will dress up as Pelagia."

I was in trouble. Just when this option fell through, Alla spent half of the account resources to bring Pelagia back to life.

However, there was a plus to this situation. He would surely agree to call the office. I explained to her the problem of visage à la Pelagia.

"You don't know my capabilities. You know little about me at all," replied Alicia and started tapping on the keyboard. "Look!"

Some photos of very pretty women appeared on the screen.

What was she getting at? Should I tell her that they are all ugly? Is that why she's showing them to me?

"Well?" I asked diplomatically, albeit with little intelligence.

"It's me!"

I looked at the monitor again and glanced at Alicia. There was a trace of triumph and satisfaction on her face.

"Are you suffering from a split personality disorder?" I risked the question.

"I graduated from a make-up course. I am older than other people from our studies by three years. I didn't get into college by first time."

"You didn't pass the exam? I don't believe it!" This information overshadowed the possibility that these super chicks are one and the same person, who was sitting in front of me and staring at me with a zombie-like look of blackened eyes.

"Sometimes you can be nice," she replied in a warm tone. "In high school I had only C's. The only A I had in P.E."

"Impossible!"

"Impossible that the C's alone, or impossible that the P.E. 's A? Anyways, that time I decided to pass for a directing program, having not watched any ambitious film in my life. Of course, I didn't get in. So I struck out on the other side to get into the film community and enrolled in a vocational course. Later I worked in the theatre for a year. But I was annoyed by these acting queens, as they often pretended to be frightened seeing me."

I imagined Alice, emerging from the darkness from between the curtains of the makeup room. In movies, usually in those places the light was dim. And suddenly a zombie walks in. Poor actresses. Poor Alicia. It's not her fault. I decided to change the subject.

"Will you call a lawyer?" I asked.

"And what will I get out of it?"

"Two cases of beer?" I took a chance.

"You still have a lot to learn about women," she sighed.

"That's what the lady from the freezer told me as well."

"How come she is still there? Do you love her? I once read a legend about a king who held the dead queen in his chamber, even though she had begun to rot and was being eaten by worms."

"I don't have any practice in disposing of dead bodies yet. Apparently, I still have a lot to learn."

"Give me the phone."

I asked Alicia to be patient for a while. I introduced her briefly into the whole affair and noted down what to ask, what to say and how to lie. Now my fate was there in the hands of this woman (I had already stopped thinking of her as a girl, probably this was caused by the three-year age difference. She was, at that moment, as old as Pelagia). The more I realized my dependence, the worse I felt.

Will I ever be one hundred percent in control of situations? Or will there always be a dependence on other people's whims? Maybe it's time to turn from a boy into an independent man?

"Don't dream about Monica now!" growled Ala from above the receiver.

"About whom?" I was surprised.

"Don't pretend. I know very well that you think about her all the time."

"I have already forgotten about her. As you can see, I have more good company," I replied, opening the door of the freezer and once again presenting Pelagia's beauty, preserved by time, botox and the coldness of the device.

"Hello, this is Pelagia!" Ala had apparently already reached the office. "What do you mean which Pelagia? How many Pelagias did you expect to call you this week?"

My colleague pretended to be outraged, at the same time trying to read something from my scribbles. Well, yes. I could have tried harder with my writing. We could also practice for a few times the calling scene.

"Yes, that's exactly me. I do not trouble myself personally, because my aunt, bless her, did not belong to the rich. A box? Do you say that the whole inheritance is in the box? Tell me, do I have to go personally to get it? Maybe you'd better send it by mail. My aunt, as you can see, was not a generous one. So what, if it's heavy. What kind of jewelry? Do you think there would be jewelry in the shoe box she had packed? And what kind of box is it? Cheap one from the supermarket? You see! How could she afford expensive jewelry? What do you mean by the conditions? Conditions to get a shoe box? She has been treated for neurosis, but this looks like a fatter case to me, although I shouldn't speak poorly of the deceased. What are these conditions?"

Alicia grabbed a pen and passionately scribbled something on a piece of paper for several minutes. She made weird faces while doing so.

I hoped that she wanted to scare me and that it was not a genuine expression of astonishment mixed with amazement.

"How much time do I have to fulfill these conditions? For two months? That's good. It may take some time... Ha, ha. Sir, do you really find it funny? I will try to face the challenge.... Although without this box I also lived well... I cannot temporarily appear at the office, I have asthma... What do you mean you will come to me... Sir, I have a mess in the apartment.... Why are you interested in my refrigerator? My aunt wrote that I cook well? Well I know it was a conversation not on the phone, but you could have stated this before... Sir, if you fall for nice voices, then you will not go far, at most to a psychiatric hospital... Sorry, that's my sense of humor. In three days, come. Yes, I will cook you pastries and red borscht."

Ala hung up.

"Pastries!" I only groaned.

"And borscht," added Alicia. "Don't forget the borscht."

"We have to get rid of the body."

"Do we? I only have to run to class." Alicia rushed off, grabbed her coat and hurried to the exit.

I was left alone, not counting the company of the deceased. On the table there was still a piece of paper, carelessly folded by Alicia. Conditions.

What could these be? Was it a chance to prolong the meeting with the lawyer? What was his name, anyway? Why did he answer the phone himself rather than the secretary? And what was the matter with the pastries? Maybe Alicia didn't call anywhere, but just wanted to make fun of me?

Who can understand women? I certainly didn't yet.

I straightened out the piece of paper. From what I managed to read, there were the following conditions.

To work for a few months as a maid.

Work sixty hours of volunteer work, preferably among the homeless.

Send signed letters and apologize to all victims of denunciations.

Rent one room to a couple for at least six months.

To work for one month as a cleaner.

To work for one month as a kitchen helper.

A series of scribbles followed, and I was no longer sure if these were my notes or Alicia's handwriting.

Who would agree to such humiliating conditions? Certainly not Mrs. Pelagia. I got to know her too well. She had her pride and unjustified sense of superiority - perhaps no one had kicked her out of college, as happened to me, or there was nothing similar that happened to her that would make her feel an insignificant person. Although, knowing Pelagia, sooner the rector would have to leave his post than she would have to resign from her hypothetical studies. How did her aunt know about the denunciations?

Were they close enough together so that Pelagia confided to her about her foul deeds?

On the other hand, she told me about it right at the beginning of our acquaintance, so maybe she didn't hide her "hobby" much. Is it possible to give up this inheritance? Pelagia would certainly not be interested in the 'mysterious riddle' in the shape of the cheap shoes' box.

But why did Jan Metlicki kill my sponsor? I was very curious, but at the same time I did not want to satisfy this knowledge.

Sometimes the less one knows, the better one sleeps - as my mother used to say when, puzzled, I asked why she wasn't interested at all in my activities going on away from home. She was basically right, although I would never have told her the whole truth about running around in socks in the snow and splitting other people's fences to have something for firewood (because we were afraid to go into the woods after drinking).

So giving up the inheritance should not be objectionable.

We will have to arrange this 'circus play' only once.

If Alicia was telling the truth about her make-up skills - which I doubted, she would somehow resemble Pelagia, she would sign a piece of paper waving her rights to inheritance, and I would be able to live long and happily in the apartment of my deceased sponsor.

Suddenly I remembered that, after all, I had seen Ala's ID card many times and she wasn't three years older there at all. Surely, I would have noticed something like this. Besides, she would not have had such a high scholarship if she hadn't applied right after high school, continuing her education. There were probably rules like that for children from an orphanage. Or maybe she wasn't from an orphanage? Certainly something didn't stick in this whole story. At some point Ala must have lied to me.

Why did she do it? Was she a mythomaniac? Who truly is this girl? And are these legal conditions true, or is it another invention of hers? Did she actually get through to the lawyer's office? After all, phones are now answered everywhere by secretaries.

Suddenly my phone rang. It was Alicia.

"They're kicking me out of college," I heard through sobs.

"Ala, what games are you playing?"

"I lied a little in the papers."

"This doesn't surprise me at this point ." I already wanted to give her a little lecture on honesty, but just then my gaze rested on the freezer and I changed my mind.

"There is still some wine left. Come by."

"Don't be scared," I heard through the sobs. "I look like a zombie because my mascara smudged."

I put the phone down and opened the cabinet to pull out the wine. I didn't find a single full bottle.

They were all standing in a row, with corks inside, but they were empty. Had Alicia been drinking all night? Fortunately, in the lounge there was still Pelagia's whiskey. I checked the label. It was intact. After all, the murderer was staying here, he could add something. I wanted to send a text message to Ali to buy some soft drinks. However, I remembered that she always carries a one and a half liter bottle of soft drink with her. I went down downstairs to wait for her.

It was quiet and snowing - the first snowfall of the year. Huge flakes were falling majestically on the sidewalks. After fifteen minutes of waiting, when it had already turned white, I heard behind me a skimming sound.

It was Alicia.

"Isn't that romantic?" She snoozed, and from her nose flowed a small trickle.

"I always enjoyed the first snow. I thought, that if I made a wish, it would come true."

"You can still do it."

"I already did. Ten minutes ago."

"Well, you see! It will definitely come true!"

"It has already come true! I wished for more luck and two minutes later, a huge icicle crashed half a meter away from me!

I was out of breath with the impression. Fictionalized or not, but this story reminded me of my bad luck. What if it was me walking down that street?

"Are you cold?" Concerned Ala grabbed my hands and rubbed them.

Surprisingly, the touch was quite pleasant. Astonished by this fact, I let her rub my cold hands for several seconds. She was the first to withdraw her hands.

"So? Are we drinking to our master's degrees?" She initiated the conversation.

Idea

"Then we'll kill the lawyer, forge the signature, take the box, and..." Alice slurred as she sipped her whiskey.

"Tell me, how to get rid of Pelagia without getting ourselves in trouble with another dead body," I said.

"Admit it," she replied, "you're the one who killed Pelagia."

I lost my voice. How could she suspect me? And what made her think that I was capable of murder? I had sometimes secretly thought of killing doctor Płonski, but then I realized that my bad luck would manifest itself in one way or another, and the lecturer was just a tool of fate.

"Ha! Only the guilty stay silent! I have an idea for disposing of the body. You'll cut her up into pieces and quietly take her somewhere to dump her. They won't have her DNA on file anywhere."

"She worked in the police. They'll have her fingerprints," I replied.

"You'll bury her hands and head."

"But I didn't kill her, and I don't have the psychological fortitude to cut up a body," I protested.

"Think about prison," she warned.

That was a slightly overwhelming vision. How many years would I spend there? They'd lock me up as a suspected murderer, in the worst cell, with the worst criminals. They'd beat me, abuse me, and then kill me, as a warning to other students (I still thought of myself as one of them). Maybe a momentary torture and slicing up Pelagia wasn't the worst idea after all?

"Ala, disposing of a body in this way is a serious matter. Who will believe me innocent if anything happens?" I said.

"Well, only the innocent keep a body in the freezer for months. Even if you explained that you didn't kill her, you'd still end up in a mental institution because such behavior isn't normal. You had a choice. You could have gone back home. Homelessness wasn't threatening you," she reasoned.

She was right. I decided to buy a saw, as kitchen knives were rather useless.

"Can I stay with you?" Ala asked. "I'm ashamed to go home, and I'll have a trial."

"You'll bring the prosecution here!" I moaned. "And you said you didn't have parents."

"We can pretend to be the couple who were supposed to rent the apartment for six months."

"How do you plan to go through with this? The lawyer is coming in two days, we don't know how to turn you into Pelagia, and now we have pastries and borscht to deal with."

"I was joking about the pastries and borscht. I got disconnected earlier."

"Earlier, when?"

"I... I don't remember..."

"And the rest was true?"

"The conditions are true, but he didn't want to give them all over the phone."

"What about the visit?"

"I'm supposed to see him in two or three days."

Suddenly, I had a criminal inspiration. Ala's friend, who falsified my residency card, could just as easily fake Pelagia's driver's license. It would be harder with a national ID card. What about a passport? Could that be done?

I reached for Pelagia's documents. The passport was new. The pages were sewn together. So, it was possible to separate them, replace the page with the photo and sew them back together. Or slightly print a new photo on the old one. It wouldn't pass customs, but the lawyer only needed Pelagia's personal identification number and photo ID to confirm if he was dealing with the right person. But how long would it take to get the photo now? An automated one was out of the question.

And I had to make Alice look a little older. How? Maybe going for heavy makeup and too-dark powder would work? Or a thick layer of powder? They would criticize her taste, but nobody would notice. Alice would turn into an old-fashioned woman from a zombie. She wouldn't be happy.

"Alice! Get dressed! We're going for a photo!"

"I'm not going anywhere. It's cold and snow is falling on me."

Alice seemed to have lost her senses a bit. She wandered with her sight around the kitchen, probably trying to sort out where she was. I decided to test my mediocre skills as a photographer and software thief. I started Pelagia's laptop and, after several minutes, managed to download a program for passport photos with preset guidelines and other bells and whistles.

Now all I had to do was smear Alice with powder. I only had the deceased's cosmetics in my apartment. Maybe it was a good thing that Alice was drunk as a skunk.

Right after taking the photo, I would wipe off the powder and she wouldn't ask too many questions, seeing her portrait sober. I took out Pelagia's accessories from the cabinet above the sink. There was a lot of it, and I didn't know which jar was for what. My knowledge, acquired from ads, allowed me to choose the cream foundation and loose powder. There was also a concealer.

When I returned to the kitchen, Alice was asleep. She didn't protest when I applied the first layer of foundation to her cheeks.

"You can make me look like a goddess, but I still won't go!" she mumbled.

When I finished my first-ever makeup, I turned Pelagia's camera to automatic mode. I sat Alice upright on a chair against a white wall and lightly tapped her cheeks. A smudge of powder remained on my hand. However, there was so much of it on my friend's skin that the small blemish went unnoticed.

Alice opened her eyes just as I took the first photo, which was meant to serve as a wake-up call. The sound of Pelagia's flash lamp would have made any paparazzi jealous. But now, she couldn't envy anyone anymore, except perhaps for someone terminally ill, longing for peace. But what kind of peace is in a freezer? Moreover, there have been two-person parties going on beside it lately. I wasn't particularly religious, but I knew that the deceased deserved absolute respect.

Maybe Pelagia had to pay for her betrayals? However, it wasn't up to me to decide.

The next photos were even worse. Alice crossed her eyes, smiled, which was prohibited in this type of photo, and in her case, it should be prohibited in any circumstances.

I started digging through the camera and found the function for serial shots. The sound of the mirror rapidly falling in the camera brought slight consciousness to Ala's face. I managed to get several bearable photos.

I chose the ones where she looked the most drunk - it was difficult to determine her age because of it. I comforted myself with the thought that the passport had been made eight years earlier, and knowing women, everyone knew that they wouldn't submit a current photo but one in which they looked the best.

Once I witnessed a woman in the passport queue who testified indignantly that the "forty kilograms less" photo was taken the day before. So the photo was fine. But what to do with Alice? Twenty years wasn't fifty, for sure.

Every man would notice that subtle difference. Powders and blushes wouldn't deceive anyone from a distance of several dozen centimeters. Simulate plastic surgery? With Ali's ugliness, a lawyer could propose filing a suit for disfigurement. And how would my friend explain it then?

Besides, there would be no explanations.

Her "what she thinks about him" speech would ruin the entire intricate plan. Wait a minute. What plan? There was no plan yet. And there should be, unfortunately, I was supposed to be the author. I had no pack of specialists to help me, as was the case in movies about grand planning, usually thefts.

I had only my not-so-specialized brain because I couldn't count on Ala, who was dizzy with alcohol. Besides, it's better if she doesn't know the details. She'll just wake up, and Pelagia will be gone. I brewed myself a strong coffee, cleared the table, put a clean sheet of paper and a pen on it. I decided to brainstorm and come up with twenty ways to get rid of the dead woman's body. This seemed to me the most important thing at the moment.

After a short moment of reflection in front of a blank piece of paper, I decided to strengthen my coffee with a splash of whisky. This was probably a mortal sin among both coffee connoisseurs and whisky lovers, but I didn't have to explain myself to anyone, especially since I had the status of a student with a 'wolf ticket'. My destiny was probably absinthe, so innocent coffee with whisky shouldn't offend anyone. Besides, who would be offended? Apart from my parents, nobody cared about me and nobody thought about me, which was very convenient in this situation.

After coffee with whisky, it was time for a few cups of tea with whisky. I added cloves, freshly squeezed orange juice, a bit of ginger, and honey to them. After the fifth tea, the list was half done.

"HOW TO GET RID OF PELAGIA FROM THE FREEZER"

Take the body out in one piece, put it in a large travel bag, and throw it away in a large garbage container - ruled out because a homeless scavenger could easily find the body, and someone would certainly recognize the victim.

Put the bag with Pelagia in the luggage compartment at the station - ruled out due to numerous cameras and the fact that the body would be quickly found.

I could execute option one, distorting the face and fingers of the victim beforehand and removing her teeth.

With Ala's help, I could take the body out and bury it somewhere in the woods - difficult to execute due to the freezing temperatures.

Following Alicia's advice, to chop Pelagia into pieces, preferably a few centimeters long, and throw them into different trash cans - difficult to implement, as I suddenly realized there were few trash cans in our city.

Tie something heavy to the body and throw it into a nearby reservoir - unethical, as it was a drinking water reservoir.

Hire someone to dispose of the body - I couldn't afford such services, and I could be harassed later.

Sending the body to doctor Plonski, along with a month's supply of lard - after a few months, I remembered his shopping list - was too risky, and I would immediately become the main suspect.

Sending the body on a long sea journey, as an anonymous package - unrealistic in a bureaucracy-heavy society.

Dissolve the body with some chemicals, for example with acid - I wasn't too good at chemistry and searching for the appropriate methods on the internet seemed risky to me.

Burn the body somewhere - it would probably take a long time and there would be some evidence left, and I couldn't watch over the last flames of Pelagia for fear of getting caught in the act.

Drop the body off at a sausage factory to be ground up - it's not very ethical, but I would get revenge on all the students. There was one such factory nearby, but of course the task posed technical difficulties, such as how to break into the factory, etc.

Cut off Pelagia's head and hands and mutilate them properly, pull out the teeth and bury them in the nearest forest with a deeper layer of soil and the body... throw it in the trash or...

Bury Pelagia's whole body in a cemetery. From what I understood, there was no monitoring in cemeteries. Few people also stayed there at night. Of course, the living could move around, but it was risky, someone might want to exhume the body (I only considered "fresh" graves, without gravestones yet), and then Pelagia's teeth could be used for identification.

Do nothing and continue to live with Pelagia in the freezer until all the issues are resolved and I can move out.

At this point, I realized that I was compromised anyway. The neighbors had seen me several times. Actually, one for sure, but the rest probably sat in their windows all day. After the body was found, I would become the main suspect.

The police would send out search warrants, show my profile in a criminal program that my mother always watched. Would I have to play the Pelagia game for the rest of my life? Or maybe ask my mother to play the role of Pelagia? She was around the same age.

I had already had my tea with alcohol and was slightly high, so I decided to check online methods for getting rid of bodies. In case of anything, I was going to explain my interest in forensic medicine, criminology, or sudden passion for joining the police force - which anyone would believe, as the short period of employment and early retirement tempted many daredevils to choose this profession.

Worse, if it ended with a house search. With Pelagia's body, I would have to claim that I wanted to learn about the methods of disposing of bodies from an autopsy and then spend the rest of my life in a mental institution.

As Alice once told me, those who don't take risks don't really live. So, I entered "how to get rid of bodies" in the search engine. A suggestion came up to search for "how to effectively get rid of bodies," and I didn't reject that option.

As I thought, the method of dissolving the body using chemicals, specifically caustic soda, was at the top of the list. Allegedly, it was possible to buy it without any problems in wholesale stores and chemical shops, as the law banning its sale had been lifted.

I read about making the solution, and in home conditions, it was not possible to achieve the required boiling temperature, which could extend the entire process by a few more hours. But what did a few hours matter after spending so much time next to the corpse? The chemicals couldn't dissolve the teeth and bones, which the guide to disposing of bodies advised to crush to make it more difficult to determine their origin if found. The resulting liquid after dissolving the body was supposed to be ecologically safe and could be flushed down the sewer system.

I had no other choice but to buy chemicals, pretending it was for clearing pipes. I wondered if the chemicals would damage the surface of the bathtub, leaving a trace of my wicked deeds. It would be better if it did not arouse suspicion by its appearance. This thought came to me when I remembered a college friend's complaints about the landlord using some corrosive agents to clean the toilet in their rented apartment, which destroyed the enamel and left fecal marks on the toilet's walls. He was not my close friend, of course – I didn't have any, but a few people wanted to have a party at his place, and the poor guy cited the unsightly and unaesthetic toilet to avoid more significant damage than just the enamel – knowing the possibilities of our group's partying. I knew about these possibilities by hearsay, as Alice and I were never invited.

I didn't want to look for the chemical store's address online anymore. I found the phone book, and yes, there was such a store in our city. I acted like a maniac, wrote down the address, found a city map that Pelagia used to track down her victims' lovers and informants, and soon knew where to go. However, I was drunk, and my need for vigilance had weakened. I decided to check the price of caustic soda online because I planned to pretend in the store that I couldn't remember the name, but my mom used it for tiles. And then I almost fainted. The product was available online for pennies. How many bodies were dissolved in homemade containers?

Another reflection came to me. What if it smells? I decided to cook something terribly smelly at the same time. Yes. Suddenly, my mind started working at an accelerated pace. The chance to get rid of Pelagia became real.

Later, I would find a job and move out quietly. I saw only one neighbor because they were older people who sat in their apartments, and besides, Pelagia knew their habits and made me leave the apartment during the hours of the lowest traffic in the stairwell – yes, life with a former police woman as a sponsor was not an easy one.

Ala's snoring cooled down my euphoria. I still had to solve the problem with the lawyers. Maybe I could find a solution online? For example, by reading about the secrets of Elvis Presley's impersonators. No. My thinking was definitely going in the wrong direction. I covered Alice with a blanket and went to sleep.

Caustic soda

The saleswoman stared into my eyes so intensely that I had no problem buying the product that was supposed to dissolve poor Pelagia. I'm not sure if it helped my intentions, as I certainly made an impression. Just in case, I said it was for the shower tiles. The saleswoman gave my body a suggestive glance and chuckled. She probably pictured me in the shower.

I looked at her with the intention of showing her some kindness, but the nicotine-tainted air, her face masked with a thick layer of powder up to her chin (of course), and nearly white blonde hair did not endear her to me. My gaze must have expressed a certain disgust, as the saleswoman's smile faded and her eyes became glassy.

With a disdainful tone, she told me the price of the product. She efficiently gave me my change and started staring at the ceiling above my head with an impenetrable expression.

All I achieved was being remembered, but the connotations associated with me were negative. A scorned woman is dangerous. Maybe she will forget about me?

I rushed to the exit, making a skillful turn at the door. She watched me with a snake-like gaze, serving the next customer. Just in case, I made a small jump through the door. Birds were lurking on the windowsills, probably wanting to defecate on me, and I didn't want to allow another event that would make me memorable to others.

Landing half a meter from the exit, I felt my foot lose in contact with the ground. Unfortunately, I was relying on it to support my body weight. My ankle wobbled to the right, to the left, and then to the right again. I felt pain. In this way, with my product - thankfully hidden in my backpack - I sprained my ankle.

"Haha!" I heard the saleswoman's joyous laughter. I wanted to give her some sort of epithet, but decided to be sensible. Who knows what a scorned woman is capable of?

Other people turned out to be nicer, but that ruined my plans. A crowd had already gathered around me - I was sitting dazed on the sidewalk and only my mind was working efficiently - one of my legs was refusing to cooperate for the time being. Someone had already suggested calling an ambulance, ignoring my protests.

"I'm not insured!" I yelled, seeing phones being pulled out.

"Maybe we shouldn't call then?" The crowd began to debate the rules and the potential cost of my medical visit. Legal regulations were thrown out. Where did they know so much about this? Did I stumble upon a lawyer's convention buying caustic soda?

Exact amounts were being mentioned... And my damn leg was hurting badly.

I felt very unhappy and for the first time in several years, I burst into tears.

I started and couldn't stop. The crowd thinned out. Everyone started rushing and dispersing. I thought my howling had discouraged them. Then I saw black, worn but nicely polished shoes. Uniform trousers above them. I started praying that it wasn't a police officer in a uniform. With a loud sob - now I had two reasons to cry - I looked up. A smoothly shaved blond was looking at me with obvious disgust.

"What's going on here?" he barked in an official manner.

"He broke his leg and doesn't have insurance," someone from the crowd immediately informed him.

The policeman squatted down.

"Which leg is it, sir, because I don't see any broken bones here?" he grumbled. It was supposed to be a question, but it sounded like a reproach and a statement of fact, like "you're a poor orphan."

I showed him my throbbing foot.

"Oh, it's just a sprain," he said.

I was waiting for him to say "it'll heal in time for the wedding," but he didn't. Apparently, I didn't win his sympathy.

"Who will take him home?" he asked the remaining people. "I'm going on a missing person call. So who will do a good deed?"

"I'll call a friend, she'll come pick me up," I tried to save my skin, because the people from the crowd looked at each other and murmured excuses, and started to disperse. I didn't want the policeman to help me get to the ex-policewoman's apartment. Maybe he'd think to check the address or, worse, invite himself in for tea or ask to use the bathroom. We were alone. Out of fear, I stopped crying and got hiccups.

"Okay, sir. Where do you want me to take you? There's no Hilton in our town, so I assume you live somewhere else?"

"I don't remember..." I decided to pretend trauma and amnesia.

"Do you have any identification on you?"

When I left the house, just in case, I left all my documents behind so as not to be ID'd when buying soda. If someone became interested in my purchase and called the police, I planned to give the data of a person disliked by me. Now that plan was out of the question. The policeman would take me to the given address. And I had a war with that person throughout high school. What to do?

"I don't have any," I began rummaging through my pockets, afraid that some old student ID, like from the Sports Association, had gotten lost in there.

"So we will go to the hospital after all, I just don't know which department to take you to, whether you have a bigger problem with your head or your leg," said the police officer.

"I can't walk, and I don't think I need my head since I don't work," I replied.

"Be careful with that attitude," the police officer warned.

I waited for him to say something like "what's allowed for the governor is also allowed for you," but he apparently didn't remember the exact phrase. Or maybe he wasn't as rude as I thought he was. He lifted me up with one pull. I leaned my weight on my injured leg to keep my balance, and the pain took my breath away.

The police officer grabbed me under the arm on the side of the injured leg, and limping, I hobbled with him to the police car.

"Wait a minute, you wanted to call your friend. Maybe she still remembers you? Do you think women forget about you?" he asked, alluding to my earlier attempt to find my phone that I had left in my apartment.

"I don't have it," I sobbed, feeling like crying again.

The police officer grimaced and opened the back door of the car. After a moment, we sped off to the hospital on the outskirts of town.

The hospital had the standard green linoleum floors and walls painted with emulsion - also green up to half the height of the room. Above that, the cheapest shade of yellow ruled - not some lime or Greek lemon. The ceiling was also yellow. It was quiet and smelled like hot dogs.

I realized it was just after lunchtime, and everyone was silently digesting their modest meal. After a preliminary examination of my leg - it turned out to be a simple sprain - the doctors sent me for a scan of my poor head. I was hungry, I had the murder weapon in my backpack, and I couldn't escape. That was my plan - to get out of there as soon as possible. However, my leg was injured and refused to cooperate.

The technician operating the machine that was going to scan my brain, which had never been examined before, looked at me suspiciously.

"Why are you so scared?"

"He has amnesia," said the nurse who was assisting me.

"Maybe sister can leave him here, he's in good hands," the technician replied.

It seemed that the role of assisting me suited her well, as it mainly consisted of waiting for my turn for examination. She didn't have to run between patients and clean up those who were sicker and digesting their lunch quickly. Therefore, she only murmured a deep "mm-hmm" and didn't move from her place.

Since arriving at the hospital, I had only spoken a few words. I preferred not to stand out with my eloquence compared to other cases of amnesia, such as a burly young man with tattoos on his hands extending from his wrists to an unknown distance, and a stinky bum who smelled of alcohol. Both of them were silent.

The bum occasionally had bouts of hiccups, which caused the man with tattoos to poke him painfully since the bum was yelling curses that he cut off halfway. Among them, I looked very polite and unassuming, and my sore ankle, wrapped in bandages, suggested a heavy and pity-inducing experience.

At least that's what it seemed to me. Finally, it was my turn for the examination. Due to stress, it would be difficult for me to remember exactly how it went.

I was pushed into some kind of device - I suspected it was a tomograph. I was a bit afraid that I wouldn't be able to endure the confined space, but I felt better there because no one could see the grimaces on my face, and I could catch my breath. They probably saw my brain.

"Have you ever had meningitis?" asked the technician.

"Are you asking me?" I was surprised.

"Only the two of us are in the room. Unless you see someone else?"

"No. Only you."

For a moment, I thought about pretending to be foolish, but I preferred not to pretend to be someone else, especially in a place where it would be even harder to escape.

"So what about meningitis?"

"I don't remember anything. The only thing that comes to mind is the movie 'Rubber,' but I don't remember much about the plot, except that the tire was killing people."

"The brain tire was killing people..." - the technician immersed himself in studying something he saw on the computer and waved his hand as if getting rid of a fly.

"Maybe you could go and call Mr. Mickiewicz," he said.

For a moment, I thought it was some kind of test, checking my mental fitness and orderly thinking, but I quietly whispered the name outside.

The tattooed guy jumped up and suddenly paled and stopped, apparently terrified by his progress.

"I remember that name, but nothing else... Besides, is that even my name?"

I seriously doubted it. Unless he was a descendant of the poet who went rough. But did

I, holding a brutally murdered woman in the freezer, have any right to judge him?

Led through the hallway by a nurse (the bum and Mickiewicz had muscular male nurses as their guardians), I tried to occupy my thoughts with something.

Mickiewicz. For the past few years, I couldn't understand why the Polish national epic begins with the words "Lithuania, my homeland." I didn't believe in conspiracy theories, so I took it as a sign of stupidity and an attempt to test what the nation would swallow. The nation wanted to forget "Pan Tadeusz" as quickly as possible, associating it with a boring school reading, except for me, who, like some pervert, had read that work several times.

Just like "Robinson Crusoe " and almost all volumes of "Anne of Green Gables," which only the librarian knew about. The nurse led me to a four-beds' room where a trio of snoring could be heard. She showed me the bed and left for a moment to return with pajamas.

"You'll change and give me your clothes. I'll be right back."

I understood that this was the last moment to escape. Running around in pajamas in winter would rather be noticed, and I, with my caustic soda, still preferred not to arouse suspicion. Earlier, I was given crutches to lean on.

When the nurse left, leaving me a moment of privacy to change, I immediately threw the pajamas into my backpack and hobbled outside the room, as if looking for the bathroom. As it turned out, both were occupied, so if I was caught, I could simulate an uncontrollable need to use the toilet and that would be the reason for my wandering around the hospital.

The corridor didn't end with stairs, but turned. Through the glass doors, I entered the geriatric ward. Elevator. To ride or not to ride? I thought about all the escapes that ended badly in the elevator. In the distance, an arrow pointed to the stairs.

With a sigh of pain - my leg hurt and the stairs were a challenge for me - I headed towards them. They were empty. Everyone was using the elevator. Luckily, my sprained leg was my right one, and the handrail was on the left side.

I had support on the left side of my body. I held two crutches in my right hand and hugged the stairs with my left, descending with small hops. Three floors down, I realized I was quite close to the main exit. Pretending indifference and looking down, I went outside.

Two taxis were waiting there. I got into the first one in the row, praying that I had enough money to get to the center. I told the taxi driver a story that I had a car accident, and I came out relatively unscathed, but my friend is immobilized and waiting for some books from bookstore.

"And you probably think I'll wait for him for free outside?"

The taxi driver became angry.

"Do I look like Mother Teresa?"

"Mother Teresa is dead."

"I'm not surprised. And I want to live a little. And live well. I won't go far on mercy!"

"You judged me wrongly, I really..."

"I know you students. And the accident was probably due to drugs? Or did your parents buy you a fancy car?"

"Why are you insulting me?" I decided to defend my dignity, even if it meant being remembered.

"People like you have too thick of a skin to be insulted."

I decided to remain silent, despite cries of "the truth hurts". I got out at the bookstore and paid the taxi man the exact amount in the smallest coins I could find. The cold air refreshed me. I had two streets to cross to get to Pelagia's apartment. I was free. I wasn't arrested. I wasn't stuck in the hospital. I didn't give anyone my personal data. Nobody I knew had seen me. I had a chance to get out of this whole mess.

Thinking about how to get rid of Pelagia's body and what to do next, I arrived at the apartment in the agreed-upon manner. I threw a stone at our window as planned. Alicia looked out immediately. When she saw me, her eyes widened. I showed her the crutches and made a "T" sign with my hands, which was supposed to mean that time was running out.

I thought this gesture was well known, but Alicia didn't seem to understand. Fortunately, we had agreed earlier that she would open the door for me and we would quietly enter the apartment. So she came downstairs. Her face reflected surprise. Even for such an unlucky person, it was quite a record event. Successfully obtaining the means to conceal a crime and returning shamefully on crutches was truly bordering on some kind of fate's joke. In the apartment, I triumphantly pulled out the soda:

"I've got it!"

Last goodbye

Pelagia was thawing in the bathtub, while Alicia went to the doctor to fake chronic nerve root pain to get strong painkillers for me so that I could fully use my intellectual abilities - which I doubted would ever happen at this point - to get rid of my "sponsor's" body.

While waiting for the medicine, I dreamt of indulging in strong liquor that would alleviate my pain of existence, but firstly, alcohol could interact badly with the medicine, and secondly, I could make a mistake while handling caustic soda. My sprained ankle was enough for me, and I didn't want any additional bodily harm.

I imagined how the chemical substance would dissolve my hands, leaving me disabled.

Additionally, I would end up in prison, without hands and at the mercy of fellow inmates.

Alicia arrived without the medicine. The doctor didn't believe her story, saying that he sees several people a day for such medication, and if Alicia wanted, she could be referred to rehab. I took four regular painkillers and felt drowsy. In principle, I could afford a few hours of sleep before the body thawed from several months of freezing. However, knowing my fate, I preferred to remain vigilant. During those few hours, many things could happen. Maybe the hospital staff was looking for me, concerned about my tormented amnesia?

Maybe police patrols had my mugshot? Just in case, I preferred to stay in the apartment for the next few days. And they would undoubtedly be unforgettable days, but unfortunately, of the kind that I wouldn't be able to brag about to my descendants. While sleeping with a woman, I would be afraid to tell her about them in my dreams. However, the word "froze my sponsor" or any word "sponsor" would only lead my future partner to the trail of paid sex, and any other circumstances hinted at in the dream would become irrelevant.

"You were talking in your sleep!" Alice exclaimed.

"Excuse me?" I asked.

"You were talking in your sleep! You fell asleep in the chair!" Alice's words slowly sank in.

"Oh yeah, I fell asleep. In one of the most important turns of events in my budding life as a criminal, while thinking about sleeping, I fell asleep. What was I talking about?"

"Something like, 'I'm sorry I have to dissolve your noble bones,'" Alice replied.

"Impossible, I would have said, 'I froze my sugar momma'..." I retorted, thinking about my breakup with Pelagia.

"If I didn't know what was going on, I would think you were talking to me. You wouldn't have caught me awake," Alice said.

So fate had its way. I would never again sleep with a woman because I would fear my sleep-talking. Even if bad luck spared me, it would leave a stain. Nothing would be as simple as my previous struggles with the whims of fate. And it was all because of my desire to take shortcuts.

Or maybe it wasn't bad luck, but my character and personality? I pondered, recalling Pelagia's words. *There are several possible solutions to any situation. I never looked for them. I was only capable of coming up with one solution and following it, adjusting to the changes in circumstances that followed my chaotic actions.*

"I'd like to comfort you, but I think it's going to get worse," Alice's voice woke me up from my bitter reflections.

"It can always get worse, but the worst crap can turn into a fairy tale," I replied optimistically.

"Maybe you should report it to the police? You're breaking even worse laws!" Alice suggested.

"I'll report it soon. I have a plan. Pelagia has probably thawed by now," I said, shifting my focus to technical considerations.

Will the rubber plug in the bathtub dissolve? Most likely. I made a note to buy a new one. Will there be traces of the corrosive substance on the enamel? Apparently, soda is also used for cleaning it, so it might not be so bad. Will there be a terrible stench? And if the neighbors smell something and alert some services? These were the questions I needed to address.

Do I need anything else? I only remember the saying: "Remember, young chemist, always pour acid into water." I decided to heat up a pot of water, pour Pelagia's body with boiling water, and then sprinkle in some soda. I sent Alice to search for a metal plug with a chain for the bottom of the bathtub, protective goggles, various gloves, and a few curry sauces that I planned to cook in the kitchen to kill any potential smell. Alice returned drunk and didn't want to tell me where and with whom she was drinking.

Did she talk about Pelagia? Would anyone believe her if she did? I suspected that since I knew about her mythomania, others who spent more time with her probably didn't pay attention to her strange stories anymore. I felt sorry for the girl. Apparently, unable to draw attention to herself with her beauty, she tried to attract attention as the heroine of mythical adventures.

The water was boiling in a large pot, the metal plug surprisingly fit the bathtub, Pelagia smiled sweetly, and I armed myself with a multitude of protective surfaces, gloves, goggles... Although I had mixed feelings about Pelagia, I still felt sorry for her. No one would come to light a symbolic candle on her grave on November 1st. Or maybe no one would come even then? Maybe her resting place would be overgrown with tall grass, mowed every few years by scouts.

Thinking about my failed visits to her grave, I went through the motions like a robot, trying to break free from our lengthy companionship with Pelagia.

My supply of caustic soda could dissolve an elephant, so I mixed one third of it with boiling water and left the bathroom, turning off the light. It was late at night, but I didn't want to take any chances, so soon the entire apartment was filled with the smell of curry.

I had several jars, so it would last for cooking all night. Alicia took out some suspicious substance from her bag and said she bought it from someone and it was codeine, which would not cause many side effects. My ankle was throbbing rhythmically with pain, so I didn't resist Ala's suggestions. That was my mistake.

I woke up in the morning. The whole apartment smelled of curry, but the stove was already turned off. There was silence. However, it was one of those strange and ominous silences. I was afraid to go into the bathroom. First, I went around the apartment looking for Ala. She wasn't anywhere. The keys were hanging on the hook by the closed door.

Although I'm not a religious person, I crossed myself before entering the bathroom.

I turned on the light. A thick liquid was floating in the bathtub. So everything would be fine, except for Alicia's hair stuck on the edge of the tub. Her long, mousey locks.

"Ala! What have you done!" I whispered.

Suddenly, I felt what the concept of gnosis was. I didn't experience a sudden enlightenment or contact with a higher power, but instead I faced its messenger - death. The heavy pressure in my stomach and chest made it difficult for me to breathe. Ala is dead.

As I gazed at the locks of her hair hanging over the edge of the bathtub, it slowly dawned on me. How could she do this? Give up on life at its doorstep? And in such a gruesome manner - entering the bath with a solution in which another woman dissolved.

What possessed her? Did she take some drug? In my mind, I pledged to make it my life's mission to catch the alleged poisoner - the dealer. For the next two minutes, I imagined hacking his imagined body with a hatchet, but it brought me no relief. Maybe Ala wanted to punish me? Impossible. She was an intelligent person.

Or was she playing me all along? When I lived in the dormitory, she often disappeared for an hour or two, claiming she wanted to be alone on a walk. She would return with flushed eyes. I thought, idiot, it's from the wind. Maybe she had had enough of pretending to be strong and balanced. Maybe something inside her broke. Why did she leave me with all this mess? I thought and immediately scolded myself for my selfishness. Or maybe she was the selfish one?

"Do I look nice?" I heard Alice's voice behind me.

Without making much contact, I instinctively looked in the mirror and jumped at the sight of her. Alice had cut her hair like a boy and dyed it blonde. My reaction did not please her. She pursed her lips in resentment, which she would nurture for years to come.

"Quite lively," I finally responded as it dawned on me that it was Alicia, whole and healthy, sulking over my latest blunders.

"Ala, never do that again!" I finally shouted, pointing to her hair waving on the edge of the bathtub.

"Well, it's a bit unhygienic, but what's all the fuss about?" she replied. "You know what? What are you accusing me of! That would be very unhygienic unless I'm mistaken about your line of reasoning."

In silence, because the pressure in my stomach and chest did not diminish at the sight of Alicia, I went to the kitchen. I thought that a light breakfast would relieve the stress. I was wrong. I felt worse and worse. I felt as if there was some mythical beast lurking behind the threshold, and I sensed its menacing presence.

What I did now crossed me off the list of innocents. Keeping Pelagia in the freezer probably fell under some form of psychopathy, but sophisticated and well-thought-out disposal of the body was a more serious matter. Moreover, my deed was irreversible. I wrapped my face in T-shirts to avoid smelling the remains of Pelagia and limped to the bathroom to dispose of the solution. The body of the deceased dissolved, but the bones remained.

However, they would always take up less space when being carried out than the entire body. Like a machine, I mixed the "liquid" in the bathtub, draining it through the pipes and praying that they were not made of some lightweight plastic that the soda would corrode, causing Pelagia to flow into individual apartments for posthumous visits to the hated by her neighbors.

At the same time, I was observing myself from the side. Here I am, a humanist, believing in the good condition of the human individual, mixing the remains of a body in a bathtub. I felt the urge to take a break, but my anxiety was stronger and urged me to act. Who knows, in a few minutes, someone might knock on the door? The liquid level was dropping, and I felt myself sinking into depression. The kind that doesn't let go for years.

Furthermore, I couldn't confide in a future therapist about what was troubling me, what had shrouded my twenty-something-year-old soul in darkness. I would keep the so-called corpse in the closet. And if Alicia blabbed to someone? Perhaps it would be better if my morning assumptions were correct and I got rid of the two bodies now?

A shiver ran through my body, and the ladle I was using to stir the mixture in the tub sent several milliliters of liquid in the direction of the window in a beautiful arc. I wanted to cry, but I couldn't afford that luxury.

First, Pelagia had to go on her final journey to the sewage treatment plant. I watched with terror as my personality changed. Would I be capable of enjoying my friend's death? I remembered my reaction to seeing her hair. Maybe there was still something human left in me? I felt a slight relief. The pressure in my stomach decreased together with the liquid level in the tub.

The enamel soda had etched into the old scratches, deepening them. I managed to remove Pelagia's remains from them. So the first stage of my plan, surprisingly, went smoothly, despite being the riskiest move I had ever made in my life. Maybe luck really does favor the bold?

Perhaps my shallow decisions did not produce the desired results because they lacked ambition? But will my fate allow me to be bold?

In essence, my further plan excluded other solutions. I had to become a good actor, rehearse the lines with Alicia, so that even when drunk, she would stick to the version of events we had chosen.

Ah, yes. Alicia drinks too much. She'll have to cut down. Although why should she change her life just because I decided to get rid of someone's corpse? Why should she bear the consequences of it? And how did that horrible experience affect her?

I gathered Pelagia's bones into a baking container from the 70s. Its diligent casing guaranteed that it wouldn't dissolve under the influence of the cooled remnants of chemicals that permeated my sponsor's remains.

I put the baking container away, and scrubbed the bathtub. Returning to the kitchen, I didn't have the courage to look Ala in the eyes. I sat at the table and covered my face with my hands.

"I found a job advertisement," Ala spoke up after a moment of mutual silence. "You need a cover so that you have some, even meager, income from somewhere. The bone will heal in a few days. In the meantime, we'll get rid of the remains and do as you planned."

After a few days, Pelagia's bones, crushed with a hammer, rested under a giant oak tree we found in the forest surrounding the town. That's all we owed her.

I felt a slight relief that her remains didn't end as dramatically as her body. The job turned out to be irrelevant. We cleaned the apartment, deliberately didn't call lawyers about the inheritance – or maybe even forgot about them a little.

In the morning, we searched the newspapers for work. Of course, we couldn't find anything suitable from the small ads. The internet was the same. A week after getting rid of Pelagia, my bone healed. I decided to move on to the next stage of the plan as quickly as possible.

Preparations

I cleaned the apartment several times a day, and the bathroom a dozen times, in preparation for getting rid of Pelagia. Once I was sure that my fate was delaying further blows, I reported Pelagia as a missing person to the police.

I thought long and intensely about how to handle the situation. If I were asked about my relationship with the missing person, what could I say? That I sublet a room from her? I had no source of income. I wasn't studying or working. That I was her kept man? I would immediately become the main suspect in an unexplained disappearance, the apartment would be thoroughly searched, and since I had no experience in covering up a crime, an experienced policeman would surely find something.

I decided to come up with a tearful story that Mrs. Pelagia took me in from the street when I was begging for food, in the cold and frost, or when I played at being a bootblack. But what if they check with the homeless people? They know each other well, and they certainly wouldn't forget the story of the pitiful ex-student taken in by a kind-hearted woman. Besides, such things never happen.

I had to let go of that version of events. Maybe I was working as a maid for Mrs. Pelagia? That was a bit of a stretch too.

All I could do was hope that the neighbors may have seen me, but hadn't noticed me staying permanently at Pelagia's. I could say that I was visiting her and that recently she decided to sublet me and Alice the apartment to fulfill one of the conditions for receiving the inheritance.

I assumed that Alice didn't exaggerate too much when summarizing the conversation with the lawyers. However, every day I lost more and more trust in her. She disappeared in the morning, reappearing late in the afternoon, without explaining these absences. Finally, I decided to ask her about it.

"But I go to college!" She protested. "Do I have to give it up for some criminal?"

This hurt me doubly. First, the story about being kicked out of college was fabricated, and second, she hit my sore spot perfidiously. I pretended not to be upset.

"You recently mentioned something about forged papers, that you're supposedly from an orphanage, or that you have an uncle who runs a grocery store, but you don't know him..."

"Well, you know what? I come from an intellectual family. I would never brag about someone from the so-called lower class."

"Ala! What are you talking about? You lived in a dorm! That's where people with low incomes go."

"Or those who will pay a bribe" slipped out of her mouth.

Again, I didn't know where I stood. Which story is true? Which Alicia is real?

I felt sadness overwhelming me. By getting rid of the body, I felt dirty and worthless. I thought that at least Alicia, despite her slight involvement, remained a noble person.

But here were lies upon lies, stories like from a melodrama. What story will satisfy the police? I decided to conduct a mock interrogation with her, playing the role of a police officer.

"Who was Pelagia M. to you?"

"My sponsor."

"Ala, don't be silly."

"She paid me to deceive the lawyers into thinking I lived with her."

"Why would Pelagia M. deceive anyone?"

"It was about some inheritance."

"Would you gain anything from Pelagia M.'s death?"

"Yes. Then Matt would become my lover."

I blushed. Finally, she said it. It was supposed to be a joke, or maybe a threat to answer the police that way, but she made it clear that she wasn't interested in me only platonically.

"Do you have any more questions?" Alicia asked.

"Would you be capable of murder?"

"Of course, like anyone!"

"Ala! What are you saying?"

"Well, it's true, but no one admits it."

"Well, I don't know. After disposing of the body, I have a guilty conscience for a few years, and if I really killed someone..."

"But how do you know what your reaction would be then? Maybe you would like it?"

"Probably not, Alicia. Probably not. And please, don't talk like that to the police. It's a serious matter. We could end up in prison. In separate prisons. You to the women's, me to the men's."

Alicia rolled her eyes.

"Let's try again. Who is Matt to you?"

"Who is Matt? I don't know."

"It's me, Ala."

"I know. I pretend I don't know in front of the police."

"You don't have to pretend that, Ala. Who is Matt to you?"

"He's a friend from school. Very intelligent, very funny, and he always helped me with various things..."

"What kind of things?" I tried to remember any help I had given to her, but unfortunately, it only worked in one direction. She always helped me.

"Different things. For example, when I didn't like someone, he beat them up and extorted money from them, and when I didn't have enough money for my scholarship, he stole food from the store..."

"Which stores did he steal from?" I thought maybe a detailed question would throw Alicia off her fabrication track.

"Mainly from Biedronka. Yes. Mostly there. He paid for half of the groceries and took the rest in his backpack. When the alarm went off, everyone saw the shopping bag and waved him through, thinking it was a device malfunction."

"What food products did he steal?"

"Chocolate... No, I don't eat chocolate..."

"I got you!" I exclaimed triumphantly. "You made a mistake in your statement."

"Do I have to stick to that statement?"

"Ala. Did that blonde color hurt you? You have to tell the truth, omitting the criminal elements. We have known each other since college. Pelagia is renting us an apartment to get an inheritance. We're a couple of clueless students. Pelagia went somewhere, but didn't come back after two weeks as promised, so we reported her missing. They'll put her in the missing persons register and that's it."

"I think it's not that simple. They have to find at least one small hook on us, otherwise it will be too stretched. We have to be like real, living people, not some saints."

"Alicia, did you drink something?"

"Four beers, I think I can, since I'm an adult?"

"Ala, real people don't say anything to the police about themselves. They don't give in. They even lie to their face in court. And that's called 'normal behavior.' If you start blackening me, they'll ask if you have some grudge against me."

"Well, of course I do."

"Let's start with Pelagia. Who was Pelagia to you?"

"She was like an adoptive mother to me. She fed me, gave me money for branded and non-branded clothes…"

"Where did you buy those clothes?"

"At the mall… at the market…"

"Why are you wearing old clothes then, when you have plenty of new ones?" I triumphantly aimed at the worn, gray sweater she was wearing.

"Firstly, I just came back from college, and I don't want others to envy me, and secondly, I didn't like Pelagia. Isn't that normal? There are times when we don't get along with our own parents."

"And how did you meet Pelagia?"

"Through Matt, who was her lover. She bought me clothes in exchange for me leaving him alone, because she was jealous."

"So she didn't really act like a mother to you, but had her own interest in it?"

"Who?"

My ankle has already healed, so I was able to hurry to the nearest store to get four beers. Two for myself and two for Ala. I felt that this whole situation would push me towards alcoholism.

I wanted to be like a Buddhist monk, insensitive to the blows of the outside world. Except that monks are isolated from this world and have never encountered such crazy people as Pelagia or Ala on their path. So I rushed for alcohol, thinking that I would drown my fears, sorrows, and growing depression. And that I would be brave enough to call the police and report the disappearance.

As I ran out of the tenement, a guy in a black coat stood on the other side of the street. I didn't pay attention to him. He was probably waiting for someone. A lot of people were here, after all, it was the city center. As I returned with the rattling beer in my backpack, the guy was standing by the tenement door, staring at me stubbornly, as if wanting to start a conversation. I lowered my gaze and barely managed to aim the key at the lock.

"Do you live here, sir?" the guy asked.

"Yes, I rent a room," I said and wanted to end the conversation there.

"I'm very sorry, do you know Pelagia?"

I was afraid to look him in the face, so I didn't remember his look. I thought that hours of preparation had made me resistant to police attacks, and here a simple passerby throws me off balance. Or maybe he was a policeman? It's better to stick to the made-up story.

"Yes. I rented a room from her. She's not at home, she left."

I decided not to share the news of the disappearance with a stranger, as I thought that this is how someone who doesn't raise suspicion should behave, someone who behaves naturally in this distorted story.

"That's far and for a long time, isn't it?"

"Are you planning to break into the apartment?" I pretended to be outraged, but the thin falsehood that came out of my throat didn't make me look like a tough guy.

"I had the pleasure of being in it recently. Please give my regards to Pelagia."

I struggled with the key, as it suddenly stopped fitting - usual thing in such situations. The man snorted seeing my panicked efforts and walked away.

I thought about how it would be if I started following him. Unfortunately, I could only think about it, as I had no experience in this. Only in movies does a person being followed go somewhere without looking back.

Although I didn't look back either, to check if someone was following me. Maybe it's time to change that? But why? Should I mix up my trail on the way to the library? Truly, suspicious activity.

However, intellectuals have made several significant changes in the world, but that certainly wouldn't be my wretched person's part. Pelagia was right. I was helpless, I couldn't make active decisions, I just waited for my galloping fate. Maybe it's time to change that?

Alice in Wonderland

Junior Sergeant Bulecki had just started his night shift. He never felt called to serve in the uniformed services, but the two-year period of unemployment after completing his studies influenced a change in his attitude.

He now sat at the station, sipping instant coffee and enjoying the blissful silence. The phone was silent like never before. *May it continue like this!* thought Bulecki. *The full moon was a few days ago, so the crazies have calmed down.* At the beginning of his service, he didn't believe in these superstitions. *What does the full moon have to do with phones?* he would get irritated hearing stories from his colleagues.

After a few months, he had to admit they were right. Not that people committed more murders during the full moon. That usually happened when a certain type of the wind blew. However, during the full moon, people called for the most nonsensical and absurd things. "There's a dead sparrow in front of my property. Someone needs to clean it up because why should children see it?"

"The neighbor's cat is meowing again. That scoundrel probably never feeds him."

After a few months, at the sight of a white disk on a navy blue sky, he began to feel irritated, knowing what awaits him during the long shifts. Fortunately, the full moon had already passed this month. Additionally, Advent time had begun, and it was Tuesday. These days, not much happens. The weekend was far away, so Bulecki slowly sipped his coffee.

He got up and went to the cabinet to take a book. Oh right. He lent it to Darek. He sat back down by the small telephone exchange. *What should I do?*, he thought. He checked the internet. Lately, he had been sending spicy messages to Gosia 123. He hoped that it was actually female. She posted a very sexy photo of a blonde in a tight pink blouse and a white mini skirt on the dating website. She was slim, graceful, and tanned. Her face was hidden by her hair, and only her nose was visible. Anyway, nothing special. Unfortunately, Gosia 123 did not respond to his desperate messages. Maybe it was because he didn't ask about her favorite hobby, only what color her underwear was when she posed for that photo. He didn't consider himself a big pervert. He thought it was just jokes that wouldn't hurt anyone. The girl wrote that she was 23 years old and, judging by the length of her skirt, certainly did not belong to the prudish ones.

He browsed through women's profiles out of boredom but found nothing interesting. Most were extreme cases. Either young ladies offering incredible pleasure in exchange for sponsorship or "thirsty for great, one true love" old Harlequin readers.

Bulecki loved reading books. That's why the pseudonym Alicja_in_the_Wonderland caught his attention. The girl in the photo had a slightly sad expression on her face, with average looks. But her body! She had a divine body! Gosia123 couldn't compete with her face alone next to Alicia. Additionally, from the description, it seemed that the girl's name was actually Ala. No, it's probably not for him. It looks too beautiful. Bulecki logged out of the website.

The smell of pizza reached him through the partially opened window. Probably the delivery guy passed by with it. Bulecki pulled out a flier from the pizzeria and began to wonder which one to choose. The thought of delicious crust with mushrooms, peppers, and of course double cheese made his mouth water. And then the phone rang.

"Madam, from whom I rent the room, left," Bulecki heard a suspiciously deep male voice. Thinking it was a joke, he replied:

"And what, are we looking for company?"

"Not company, just that woman," came the reply.

"There are plenty of women in the world," Bulecki said, and was about to end the conversation with a standard line about bothering the police when the caller added another line.

"After all, I know what she looks like, and I have a photo!"

Bulecki realized that he was dealing with a missing person case.

"Please call all hospitals, including psychiatric ones, first. "

"All of them? In the whole of Poland? I don't know where she went and I have nothing in my account."

"We need grounds for such a report. Usually, it is the family who informs, not students subletting an apartment. Maybe this lady has another home? Maybe she went to her lover and is having fun... Have you tried calling her?"

***

I realized that I should have made the story of Pelagia's disappearance more credible. I didn't call her phone. And yet the police can check it. They might also be able to track her phone, although it seemed like an unlikely move in such a case. But I could be wrong.

"Are you there?" I heard an impatient policeman's voice.

"She left her phone."

"She went out shopping?"

"No. She said she deserved a vacation."

"So, the trip was planned. When was this lady supposed to come back? Please also give me your name and surname and our traveler's details."

I provided all the requested information. The officer said he would make a note and gave me a reference number, then started joking about holiday love affairs. Slightly stunned, I hung up the phone.

Did I gain another few days, or even weeks? When should I call the police again? I decided to do it in two weeks. Some people win wars in two weeks... Ugh, what am I talking about? Probably some business maneuvers. Maybe in ancient times, they killed off the competition and covered their tracks... It was going slowly for me, but at this stage, I preferred not to rush events. What to do in the meantime? I haven't withdrawn any money from Pelagia's account for two weeks. She finally left and physically wouldn't have a chance to withdraw money from local ATMs. Alicia moved back to the dorm and stopped answering the phone.

During these two weeks, obsessive thoughts of death haunted me. Pelagia didn't foresee hers. I had nightmares that our city was occupied by unspecified types. And at the end of every dream, I walked towards execution, wondering what would happen to my personal calendars where I recorded my daily activities.

I said goodbye to life in these nightmares and felt regret for what was unfulfilled. Is this really the end? Will I never read a book, go to college, or start a family? I woke up before the first alarm and slowly became aware of my bamboo surroundings. Oh, how I wanted to move out.

However, I had to occupy my mind with something. I could no longer focus on studying and preparing for university. Finding the murderer - that could solve a few things. I was quite involved in this matter, but in the end, I didn't kill anyone. I just stored the body in the freezer and then got rid of it with chemicals. Sounds beautiful. Oh well.

I guess I'll have to put the idea of studying on hold. Maybe leave the country? But for what reason? I saved some of Pelagia's money, but it wasn't an emigrant-worthy sum. And where would I go? My English was mediocre. I could only say in Russian that I didn't understand anything, but I wouldn't choose Russia anyway. Knowing my luck, I'd be gone within the first ten hours of setting foot on shaky, Russian ground, and in a way that would undermine my masculinity.

I only knew sports vocabulary in French because my dorm neighbor once got hold of a website on the internet where he watched boxing and football matches commented on by snail enthusiasts.

Move to the seaside? Hide in the mountains? Or somewhere near the eastern border where only country bumpkins would be interested in me? No, it's not that simple. A newcomer everywhere raises a sensation and is a mystery - why did he leave? Why did he come to that particular place? Who is he? What does he do? And, of course, everyone would be interested in my marital status as well.

The sound of the phone ringing was so unexpected that at first, I thought it was the alarm on the radio. No one had called me for a good two weeks. The last conversation I had was about the possibility of changing my electricity supplier - some woman from the sales department called me. I preferred to call my parents first. Surprised, I didn't manage to answer in time.

It was Ala. I quickly called her back.

"So, are they letting you out of jail?" There was a sour tone in her voice.

"They don't want to search for Pelagia."

"Oh my God! What a poor woman!"

"Are you joking?"

"I really feel sorry for her. The donkey with the lame leg wasn't interested in her…"

"You mean the dog."

"A dog would have shown interest in its owner. For example, it would bark or run for help. But a donkey would probably eat her bamboo furniture."

"Ala, I have more time now to deal with the whole situation. I've decided to find the murderer. He must be found!"

"Him or whoever… By the way, why do you think it's a man?" I briefly told her about the SMS and phone calls before Pelagia's death. Alicia gave me a short lecture on sexist narrowing of the circle of suspects.

"Alicia, I'm telling you, it had to be him," I said. Ala started grumbling about statistics. I asked her to come and talk in person. I didn't want to discuss everything over the phone. If Pelagia's case aroused interest, my conversations could be bugged. I imagined a policeman choking on his meal while listening to Alicia's arguments with her tendency to use difficult terms instead of ordinary words.

They probably would have to hire a specialist or invest in a dictionary. After a few conversations with her, I already made that purchase, and the book turned out to be my best friend. Alicia once noticed my dull expression and since then she tried to express herself more in a human way in direct conversations, but sometimes she still got carried away over the phone.

"Explain something to me. Why are you looking for that bastard only now?"

"I can't explain it. Those few months were a nightmare. Just like in a nightmare, you can't escape, I was helpless."

"You're bullshitting. I'll be there soon." I heard the agreed signal on my cell phone fifteen minutes later.

Did she take a taxi? I hurriedly put on my four-season Gore-Tex jacket with a lining and, trying to step as quietly as possible, went downstairs. It was quiet. Large, single snowflakes were slowly falling from the navy blue sky at this time of the night. There was no wind, so they majestically swirled in the air, not hurrying to settle on the concrete sidewalks and disappear.

"You see!" I pointed at the snow falling in the square.

"It didn't sound romantic…"

"Even snowflakes die! Look, a few seconds and they melt."

"You're not fit for philosophy either. Let's go for a walk!" she decided.

"I'm not going anywhere farther than the convenience store," I muttered.

"You're blabbering about death, yet you died yourself several months ago, along with Pelagia. Even a simple walk is too much for you. We're going to the cemetery!"

"I prefer the park."

"A corpse was found in the park yesterday."

I looked at her carefully. Was she making it up again? Or maybe not? A dead body was an anomaly in this sleepy town. At least for the public. I was stronger, having lived under the same roof as the deceased for several months. Maybe a new case would occupy the police enough not to bother with such a trifle as the disappearance of an elderly woman? But is it true?

Or maybe these murders are related? For example, by the killer? Maybe it's a serial killer? Unfortunately, Alicia didn't know the details. She didn't know whether the victim was a man or a woman, and whether the perpetrator had been caught.

"Why are you asking so many questions?" she snapped at the sixth one. "Do you have too much space in your freezer?"

I pulled my worn-out hat out of my pocket and put it on my head.

"First, the convenience store!" I decided.

"Where did you grow up when you used such language? Convenience stores were in the PRL."

"In the countryside! I even helped spread manure in the field once."

"Ew!"

"And who are you? I don't hide my origin, my flaws, or my vocabulary. I'm not ashamed of my parents. They work hard." I sighed.

I couldn't get Pelagia's money anymore. That meant paying off the first year of tuition debt again was not possible. It would hit my family's pocketbook hard. Fortunately, I had set up transfers from her account to ensure that all payments and rent were paid with Swiss clock precision.

Or maybe I should use a more modern term? My lack of social skills among peers was showing. I used vocabulary acquired from my parents, grandparents, and literature.

"My parents left. They're in the States."

"Girl, you should write books. Every time I hear a different story from you. Maybe you live in parallel worlds? But how many of them do you have in your case? Dozens!"

The woman at the supermarket checked our IDs before selling us alcohol. For a moment, I thought about giving up on the purchase. I calculated how much I drank in the last two weeks and felt disgusted. It was definitely too much. As I was leaving the store, I thought that maybe I wasn't paying all of Pelagia's bills. Now it was irrelevant. Pelagia left and disappeared, and I was just a poor student renting a room.

Ala moved out to the dorm, so I didn't have to tell the police about her colorful personality - thus preempting the various made-up stories she would have served them. Or maybe there's something wrong with Alicia's head? I looked at her carefully.

"What are you staring at?" she grumbled. "I'm not the Mona Lisa to be contemplated like this. Besides, whether I'm uglier or prettier than her, at least I'm alive. And I intend to enjoy life."

"How?" I asked.

"I have a plan. I'll have a private plane that I'll fly around the world and so on."

"And how do you plan to achieve that after studying cultural studies?

"I'll sing." Alicja took a breath and started singing some song I didn't know, off-key.

"So, how was it?" she asked.

"It didn't go very well," I replied honestly. "But if you work on your voice, you'll probably succeed."

"What, you mean I sing badly?"

"A little like a crow imitating a skylark's trill."

"Gotcha! I was joking about singing. At least I know you're honest. Let's go to the cemetery. I want to show you something."

"It's cold and I'm down."

"You'll get over it."

It was dark in the cemetery. The snow had stopped falling and melted. The cemetery lanterns were turned off.

Only in the distance, in the so-called new part, could a faint glow of candles be seen. That's where Alicia took me. Stumbling over graves, I got a few bruises. I was angry with my friend. Really, on All Saints' Day, there are more candles to admire.

"First, have a drink," suggested Alicia suddenly, halfway to the lit-up grave.

"At the cemetery? Have you gone mad?" I protested.

"It will do you good," something in her tone made me stop objecting. After a few sips of wine, I lost my patience with Alicia. Yes, the mulled wine warmed me up and made me feel better, but it would have tasted much better in a pub. Not in a cemetery and certainly not in winter.

Gradually, my eyes adjusted to the shadows and half-shadows of the night. Alicia resumed our walk. I thought it would be better, but I still stumbled over something.

"Ala, it would be a better idea to light a fire somewhere instead of warming up by someone's grave."

"Wait until we get there."

Our destination was illuminated by dozens of candles, and there were many wreaths. It was clear that the person buried there had recently died and was popular.

"You probably want to tell me that someone young died, blah, blah, blah, and I still have my whole life ahead of me."

"It's Pelagia."

"Are you joking?"

"I knew you wouldn't believe me, that's why I wanted you to see it with your own eyes."

"From where? How..." I cleared the wreaths covering the plaque with the deceased's details. It was Pelagia. I sat heavily on the neighboring grave.

"Hey, someone's lying there!" Alicia reacted. She also said something else, but her words didn't reach me.

"Maybe it's her another trick? It's impossible for there to be two Pelagia Metlicka in the same town," I said.

"Ala! Admit it honestly..."

"I knew it! I knew you would say that."

"But I haven't said anything yet."

"But you wanted to. Don't accuse me of anything! Maybe I'm ugly, but I always tell the truth!"

I choked on the hot mulled wine and then started laughing hysterically. I couldn't stop.

"Ala!" I said after a while, when my stomach hurt from laughing. "Your statements are always logical. Well, almost. Sometimes I wrote down the tautology of your statements."

"Of course they're logical!"

"According to tautology and logic, they're true. But there's not a shred of truth in what you say over days, weeks, months."

"Because if I'm ugly, I'm a liar?"

"How many stories have I heard about your family? About uncles who were shopkeepers, parents who were lawyers, or immigrant parents?"

"And you think it's easy to live without family history? You probably heard at family gatherings about the travels of your uncles, grandparents, the life of your parents, uncles, and aunts. And me? Pass me the wine... Anyway, why am I explaining this to you? It's like trying to show colors to a blind person."

"Let's just say I got the metaphor," I said after a moment of thought.

"What will you do with that information?"

"I don't know. I know it's cold, I'm feeling down, and I'm allergic to the dead," I muttered.

"You don't seem to be taking it too hard," she said surprised.

"For one, I'm in shock, and for two... I'm so down that I've become indifferent to everything. Shall we go back?"

On the way back, wanting to detach myself a little from the gloomy and slightly absurd reality, I told Alicia about creating a dating account with her photo. Alicia asked me for the password. Despite the cold, her face turned red. She was probably upset.

"You asshole!" she said.

Waking up from lethargy

A month had passed since the dissolution of Pelagia's body. Winter was still going on. However, despite the snow, cold, and lack of sunshine, I felt a hope sprouting in me for a change for the better.

Slowly, I was awakening from lethargy. First of all, I decided to find the murderer. I also had to check who Pelagia from the cemetery was, get rid of lawyers, and preferably leave the city and forget about the whole story.

The latter was tempting, but I convinced myself that the shortcut leads to bigger troubles. In every thriller, everyone immediately looks for the perpetrator of the crime. Why was it different in my case? What terrible thing must be in my character that I am helpless even in the face of such dramatic events?

After visiting the cemetery, I hid with a notebook. I wrote down the clues and leads, of which there were few. After a few hours of philosophizing and pouring out my regrets over my own helplessness, I decided to start behaving like someone who would normally behave in such a situation. I called the police.

After all, I had nothing on my conscience, hypothetically.

"That missing lady has been found!" I shouted hoarsely into the phone as soon as the operator answered.

"Which one? Please give me the details."

"The one I live with. A friend found her, but in the cemetery."

"Do you need an ambulance?"

Seeing that the conversation was leading nowhere, I took a breath and gave Pelagia's details, as well as describing our discovery at the cemetery.

Judging by the silence on the other end of the line, the police officer did not know what to do with this phantom. Finally, he spoke up:

"We will pass it on. Do you want to add anything else?"

"Nothing to add, but will someone inform me about the results of the investigation?"

"There is no investigation yet in this case."

"Will someone let me know who Mrs. Pelagia Metlicka from the cemetery is and whether she is my landlady?"

"We're sorry, but no. This information will only be available to family members."

I said goodbye politely and hung up. I put one hundred zlotys into my wallet and went to the rectory to which the cemetery belonged. To my surprise, I found the priest in his office.

"I heard about the loss of someone and I am ready to order a mass for their successful afterlife, I just wanted to make sure it's the person I'm thinking of."

The priest's gaze seemed to sharpen. He looked around nervously, as if making sure he wasn't on a hidden camera.

"You're talking about Mrs. Pelagia. Please leave! I've had enough of this! Are you checking up on me? The Church is not as weak as you think. I also have strong connections..."

"Umm" I made an unintelligent sound. Apparently, it was a bigger matter or the priest was currently possessed by some ghosts. I decided to lay some cards on the table:

"If it's the woman who rented a room to me, she disappeared a few weeks ago... I'm worried about her..."

"Are you paying the rent now?"

"I have no one to pay for it to."

"Then why worry? Do you think I'm stupid and will fall for your pseudo-student tricks? The Vatican is more powerful than you think! We reach people and we have our own people. We're still powerful!"

I withdrew from the office because the priest was so agitated that he started spitting while he spoke.

I returned intrigued. Who was Pelagia? What was this whole story about? Why was the priest so agitated and didn't want to say anything?

On the staircase, I met my neighbor from downstairs. I, of course, ignored him and didn't respond to his "good morning". The neighbor passed me and suddenly stopped in the doorway of the tenement.

"Do you still live here?" he asked.

"Yes. Did you happen to have any news from Mrs. Pelagia? She left and..."

"I was at her funeral a few days ago, but no, I didn't talk to the deceased..."

"It's impossible that it was Mrs. Pelagia! Someone would have told me!"

"Soon the heirs will come to the apartment. If you don't have a rental agreement, you'll have a problem," the neighbor chuckled and left the tenement.

Now I knew why Mrs. Pelagia didn't like her neighbors. I had to think quickly, but in my head, instead of a brain, there was a sponge.

Again, I felt that damned helplessness, the lethargy of a cowardly person. I started cursing my character under my breath. What would I do? I would probably call for help from the young woman, that is, Alicia, instead of taking some action that would result in a favorable reaction for me.

I stopped on the stairs. Where did the body of Pelagia come from if she was theoretically buried in the cemetery? Someone had to confirm her death and record it in some official registers. She probably also lay in some morgue... Who was it, since I myself had disposed of the body? Who organized the funeral? Where can I get this information?

I rushed upstairs to write down all these questions before I forgot them. I grabbed a pen, found an old notebook from my studies. The pen refused to cooperate. I took a deep breath and entered Pelagia's room.

There was a slight mustiness in the air, as in a long-unventilated room. Nervously, I grabbed one of the pens she kept on the dresser. I pulled the object too hard. The pencil case and pens tipped over, and their contents spilled out onto the carpet. I began to collect the pens. Several of them rolled under Pelagia's bed.

Remembering her fear of mice, I preferred to look there rather than risk my hand and break my fingers on some mouse trap.

It turned out that I was right. There were five traps under the bed, already slightly rusted, and some boxes. One was pink, the other black, and the third orange.

If they were ordinary cardboard boxes, I probably wouldn't have checked their contents. However, the colorful boxes sparked a little curiosity. Maybe she kept expensive shoes or bags in them? By which designer? And why did she dress nicely, but didn't go overboard with expensive purchases?

The boxes were pushed deep under the bed. I needed the help of a memorable spade to pull them out. I opened the first one. Inside was a stack of papers written in Pelagia's uneven handwriting. The one on top looked like a list of some unknown people. The next ones were probably copies of reports.

In the second black box, there were notebooks with small notes written in them. They looked like diaries.

In the orange box, I found more papers and a few stacks of hundred-dollar bills and a passport with Pelagia's photo under the name Dobroslawa Raznienska. It was a Russian passport.

Pelagia's boxes

The sound of a funeral march knocked me off balance. It was Pelagia's phone. The lawyer was calling.

"Good morning, may I speak to Ms. Pelagia Metlicka?" the lawyer seemed surprised hearing my male voice.

"Ms. Pelagia left and accidentally left her cell phone at home."

"When did she leave?"

"I'm not sure if I can provide such information," I definitely didn't plan to inform the law office about Pelagia's disappearance or her current location in the cemetery. Let them find out in two months, but not from me.

"And who are you?" the lawyer asked.

"You didn't introduce yourself either!" I retorted.

"I'm calling about a confidential matter. Please inform Ms. Pelagia that the deadline is in a month."

"The deadline for what?"

"She'll know what it's about."

For about a month, I got rid of the lawyers.

My feet were burning from walking on hot coals. I'll have to go back to my village soon. I'll work for Uncle Henrik to pay off my student loan. Maybe prison wasn't such a bad place? If only it lasted six months. That would be enough penance for me. I would have a roof over my head, food, and time to study. Pelagia's boxes. At first, I wanted to ignore them, but Alicia's recent mention and her talks that I should be more positive about life and its events made me start digging through their contents.

I started with the box of reports. It contained copies of reports and letters to the victims preceding the reports. That's what I deduced from the dates.

Everything was neatly sorted, along with notes on each person, who they are, and what they do. For a moment, the thought crossed my mind that I could blackmail these people and make a living that way, but, firstly, I was not a professional crime maker and secondly, it was immoral.

The mere awareness that I had come up with such an idea made me feel bad. Was I a bad person? What about my ability to distinguish between good and evil? I was definitely deteriorating. Life had given me a difficult challenge, and I had failed that exam.

For a moment, I wanted to put the box aside. A bell in my head rang alarmingly, telling me that I had just opened my personal Pandora's box. However, among the papers or in the diaries, there could be mentions of Jan Metlicki. Maybe I'll find the reason for Pelagia's premature death. Maybe it wasn't inheritance, but a perfidious report or blackmail that upset someone?

I knew I would find quite a mess in these papers. Not a physical mess, everything was neatly organized. Here I was about to enter someone else's hidden secrets, small crimes, betrayals.

And yet I wanted to believe that this world is a positive place. Despite my bad luck, I stubbornly believed in it. That is until Pelagia's death. If someone had told me at the beginning of the academic year that I would be living with a dead body, I would have probably called the shrinks to help him. And now I had to dig through even worse dirt. What did all these people do? And what made them the victims of an otherwise balanced Pelagia?

A murderer. It must have happened due to a frenzy attack. At least that's how it was described in the criminology textbook that I illegally downloaded from the internet. But what if they were wrong? What if someone planned this with cold blood after reading the same textbook? Maybe they wanted to stage a frenzy attack? Would they have turned off the gas then? Or did they notice that someone else was living with their victim?

I was a bad detective. I should be happy now that I found some leads that would fill the police investigation for months. But what's the point? I would be in jail by then, so the excess evidence of the deceased's despicable character only gave me a headache.

I felt like throwing the boxes out of the window. Discovering them made me decide to systematically search the entire apartment. I found two more boxes with diaries and one hundred thousand zloty in one-hundred-zloty banknotes.

After that last discovery, I felt like a hidden camera hero. It came too easy to me. I felt my face burning and my throat hurting.

And so, after finding such a pile of money, like a real loser, I went to the kitchen to drink cough syrup and soothe my sore throat. I also took my temperature. It was slightly elevated, but nothing alarming. The apartment had gotten cold, which I hadn't noticed in my search for Pelagia's private papers.

I collapsed onto a stool in the kitchen, sipping on winter tea. Was I saved? Not necessarily. Everything would have been fine if I had found the money before calling the police.

And before finding the second Pelagia at the cemetery. I would have quietly left, cleaning the entire apartment with some cleaning products to erase any traces of my rather long stay. But now?

I made a call about Pelagia's disappearance and gave the police my information.

I couldn't suddenly become rich. I felt, or maybe I was just slightly paranoid, that now I would be under surveillance.

I couldn't suddenly afford an apartment because I didn't have enough income. I couldn't deposit the money into my account.

I could only afford to live in a pile, as the eighth roommate in a student room. And they would quickly discover the money. Was I stuck in a dead end? Was I condemned to live in Pelagia's apartment?

"I have to find a job," I thought, probably as the first among the discoverers of a large sum of money.

I wanted to call Alicia, but stopped halfway through dialing her number. I remembered her sarcasm and harsh words from our last goodbye. That I still needed her help and couldn't behave like a man. She was probably right.

And she was honest. But couldn't she express herself more delicately? Or maybe that's what I needed? For someone to shake me up? On the other hand, life hadn't spared me any kicks lately, so Alicia could have held back. She made me feel like a failure. I didn't feel good about that conclusion.

Or maybe it was Alicia's money? After all, Pelagia sometimes complained that we would have to eat bread with butter for two days because she didn't have enough until her pension. Did she have such a split personality, that like in the Bible, her right hand didn't know what her left hand was doing? I decided to call my mom.

"Son, they want to take away my machines."

Mom had two sewing machines on which she worked until retirement. I felt low. I asked for the sum needed to cover my debt. Considering my sudden enrichment, although I didn't feel like the owner of that money yet, I was able to confidently tell my mom: 'Don't worry, I'll take care of it.'

I sat at my wretched kitchen table and began to ponder. Only one thought came to mind - to tell the police that I received the money as an escort.

There would be some shame, I would be even more suspicious, but this whole explanation would only be necessary if the police asked how I became the owner of the cash. I rushed to the post office and deposited the required amount into my mom's account. The lady was a bit surprised, not many people deposit several thousand zlotys.

And then I realized that I made a mistake. I could explain away those few thousand, but not several tens of thousands. That could be the main motive for suspicion of a crime. I wasn't such a great guy to extort such an amount in a few months as an escort.

I'll have to save the money and keep thinking about how to get out of my unpleasant situation without taking shortcuts.

To occupy my poor head, which had to think much more than the heads of my peers, I started reading the contents of the boxes.

Pelagia's letter

The copies of letters and reports were written more clearly, so I began reading them instead, discouraged by the Byzantine character of Pelagia's writing in her journals. Or perhaps my clumsiness was showing again? I was slightly distracted, but I decided to look for the "documents" of Jan Metlicki. Unfortunately, I found nothing.

My thoughts wandered between the money on the table, Alice's words, and predicting future events. Oh, how naive I was! How could I have thought that I was able to predict the course of events?

My fate was watching over me. Recently, I read a rather optimistic piece in a book about a predicted mission to be carried out and how higher forces watch over a person until they fulfill their tasks. As for me, I was more likely to have some terrible household chore to complete, like something from the field of quantum physics, whatever that field of science is. And after receiving a negative evaluation of this chore, my life would have ended.

Pelagia often repeated a quote from one of her favorite authors: "You are what you think." With that in mind, I decided to rephrase my recent, pessimistic thoughts.

This struggle with fate is just a test, one that will toughen and strengthen me. Someday, I will find out what my "mission" is. For now, my mission was to catch the murderer.

I put the papers aside for a moment as the letters danced all over the page. What good would it do me to catch the scoundrel?

I couldn't very well take him to the police. And I didn't plan to kill him either, as he could be invaluable in case the authorities ever tried to bring charges against me.

In fact, I would have to take care of him to make sure he didn't blab or run off to another country. Who knows? Perhaps he is working on a farm in Argentina right now, seducing the owner. Does he have a family? I groaned. Why hadn't I entered his information into a search engine yet? I turned on my laptop but was met with a message about a system configuration. After half an hour of trying, I gave up and went back to browsing search results. The first letter I found was dated three years ago.

I started reading and slowly forgot about all the configurations, and even about poor Mr. Metlicki.

"Dear Sir," wrote Pelagia, "I realize how strange my hypothesis sounds. It contradicts the materials and studies you have gathered. However, Copernicus was also suspected of being a woman."

I imagined Pelagia writing those words. She probably had already smoked a few packs of cigarettes and had something to drink, wanting to share her pseudo-theories with the world.

I read on, curious about what she had come up with that time. However, in this particular paper, she focused on inventing amusing metaphors to describe the failed prophets, messiahs of knowledge, and the arrogance of scholars.

"I know that when you come across the shape of an idea, a concept, or an explanation of a phenomenon, a light bulb goes off in your head. And under the bulb is the darkest spot. This light, like a will-o'-the-wisp, leads you through a maze of theories. Everything starts to fit together like a puzzle for a three-year-old. I hope you don't swallow any of the pieces of the puzzle, like a naughty child."

I choked on my own saliva. At the same time, I felt a certain nostalgia for my "sponsor" and her brainwashing methods, which she tested on me. This nostalgia could probably be linked to Stockholm syndrome.

"When the puzzle pieces fit together, you announce your theories to the world and gain new scientific titles. It doesn't matter that the puzzle only shows a drawing of tangled wires, something where only an obsessed mind would see a suggested flower. You also make the common mistake of looking at the world through the prism of your own experiences. Experiences that are not very rich, not very valuable, and are nothing compared to the course of history."

I wonder if she ever received a response, if she sent this letter. The recipient was anonymous. At least, for me. There was no name or surname in the letter header, only a date and a polite greeting, followed by two pages of Pelagia's reflections.

I concluded that they were not very revealing, but I was curious about which theory she wanted to debunk with her tangled language full of metaphors. However, I didn't find any hint in this letter about what she was talking about. Apparently, she was referring to earlier letters.

"I kindly request to check the credibility of my hypothesis" - this polite ending surely barely crossed her fingers when she typed the words on the keyboard.

I tried to remember if she talked about something controversial. Usually, I listened to stories about the power of the mind, about the resilience of some individuals.

I couldn't remember anything about any scientific theory that would have upset her so much. I got to know her a little, so I sensed that when writing this letter, she was angry about something - probably the response or the lack of it to her previous letter. I put the letter aside.

I checked the computer. The system configuration was probably finished. Unfortunately, it started downloading updates, which were currently downloaded only two percent. I thought they would quickly go up. However, after ten minutes of staring at the screen, I still saw the same number.

The sound of Pelagia's funeral march ringtone didn't speed up the download of the update, but it certainly raised my pulse. It was already very late.

Who could be calling? The screen displayed "unknown number". Despite that, I decided to answer.

The caller didn't use any metaphors like Pelagia.

"I assume you've found the money by now?"

"What money? Pelagia left, I don't know what you're talking about."

"I thought your problem was money. You paid off your loan, you could leave. What else is keeping you here?"

"I paid off the loan with my savings," I began to explain.

"Just go somewhere far away and live so that I never have to hear about you again. Please believe me, this situation is more distressing for me than it is for you."

The sound of the disconnected call rang in my ears. The computer screen displayed that the updates had only been downloaded three percent. Who called? The police? Who else could have checked the bank transfer so quickly?

I felt suffocated, despite the ample amount of fresh, cold air flowing through the cracked window. I went to splash my face with cold water. I looked in the mirror and didn't like what I saw.

The terrified look of a scared rabbit stared back at me. Zero self-confidence. I lowered my gaze, which landed on my trembling hands. I wanted to call Alicia. Maybe she was right. I couldn't solve any problems on my own.

"You never know how you should behave. You put off making decisions until the last moment," she said.

I should handle all of this like a man, instead of calling the female every time and asking for advice. If it was a police officer... Why am I not in handcuffs right now? Why is no one accusing me? The money was on Pelagia's wardrobe. Were they there before?

Or maybe she wasn't so crazy as to eat bread and butter while sleeping on thousands? Maybe someone planted them there? Why does someone want me to disappear? Is it a murderer? Right. Pelagia worked in the police force. She might have angered one of her colleagues. They would have access to various data.

Is it possible that he obtained this information so quickly? Surely court orders are required to obtain confidential information such as commercial transactions? Pelagia has often talked about problems with capturing criminals due to this requirement. So how did this man know about my transfer so quickly?

He couldn't have obtained this data so quickly. Unless I was mistaken, courts don't work at night. Or maybe some other procedure was involved that accelerated the collection of data? Even though I lived with a police officer, I knew little about police work methods. Let's assume that it was a police officer who illegally obtained banking information. Doesn't that leave some traces? Wasn't he afraid? Or maybe the whole station or department is involved?

Did I become paranoid? Why would someone leave a hundred thousand zlotys for me to disappear? Wouldn't it be cheaper to just get rid of me?

A series of shivers ran through my body. I put on my jacket and grabbed a blanket. For the first time, I forgot about walking silently. Apparently, my footsteps woke up the neighbors downstairs because I heard persistent knocking on the floor.

I decided to call Alicia. I needed a witness. I didn't want to just pretend nothing happened without first telling someone I trusted, who would continue my clumsy investigation.

"I was waiting for your call," Alicia's voice sounded fresh, apparently she hadn't gone to sleep yet. "I'm sorry for what I said. It's normal that you don't know how to behave because you're not a repeat offender."

"Ala, do you have money for a taxi?"

"How much do you need to borrow?"

"The money problem seems to have solved itself."

"Not by itself, but I'm lending it to you. You'll pay me back when you can."

"Get in a taxi and come over. Just don't get in any of the ones parked under the dorms. And take care of yourself."

"Did all this stress make you crazy?"

"This is not a conversation for the phone," I said in a typical phrase.

"You could talk about corpses, but not about money?"

"How do you know it's about money?"

"Well, you wanted to borrow it."

"Ala, I'll see you here in fifteen minutes," I hung up.

The sound of a car engine approaching woke me up from my dazed stare at the computer screen, still showing a three percent update status.

Frustrated with the lack of cooperation, I forcefully restarted the computer. The black screen was the result of my next mistake. I slammed the laptop shut.

I decided to hide the money. Maybe Alicia suddenly came up with the idea of throwing a party at my place and invited half the academic community? I threw the bundles of money into the cupboard, just in time. I heard the sound of a key turning, which used to belong to Pelagia.

Alicia's hair was in a mess. The makeup she had applied recently was gone. The dark circles under her eyes looked very familiar now.

"Did someone call the police?" she asked.

"How do you know?"

For a moment, I felt a heavy pressure in my chest. What if Ala is in cahoots with the police? It would make sense. I was like the scientist from Pelagia's lecture. I clung to the theory that she was enchanted with me and would do anything for me. And yet, she was an intelligent woman.

Why should she get involved in such a messy situation because of a guy? There are billions, or maybe trillions of guys, I couldn't remember the exact data from geography. Surely she would have immediately told and reported everything where it was necessary. I would have done the same. So why was I still free? If the situation had taken such a turn, would the police patiently track my clumsy attempts to dispose of the body? Although they were everywhere. When I bought the shovel. When I bought caustic soda.

Nothing in this whole story made sense.

I asked her to sit down. I took out the money and threw it on the table.

"Are you involved in counterfeiting?"

"How do you know they're fake?" Another lantern lit up in my mind. Maybe the lady at the post office reported fake banknotes?

"I don't know. Where did you get so much money?"

She took out one of the banknotes and examined it carefully.

"There's a watermark, most of the security features that my uncle told me about are here too..."

"Enough with that uncle, the shopkeeper."

"My uncle is real," she insisted. "He was the only one who visited me at the orphanage. He was in prison, so he couldn't adopt me."

"Do you still have contact with him?"

"You have to solve your own problem yourself. You surely know the solution by now. And by the way, don't talk to me, just explain where you got so much money. Because no one would fall with that much money for your pimple on your nose, Mr The Keeper."

Discovery

I was reading the hieroglyphs of the deceased. The thought of her hands holding a pen and writing on those pages made me feel sick. The same hands whose bones I had crushed with a hammer on a Sunday morning, pretending to beat pork cutlets. I pushed these thoughts away, but they came back with increased force. I tried to concentrate.

"Hey, she might have discovered something," it was late at night and we were huddled over the found materials.

"Too bad she didn't foresee her death," said Alice.

"Listen to this," she started to read. "I believe that methods of encrypting messages using sudoku are already very outdated, although they may still be useful."

"What is sudoku?" – Ala interrupted the reading.

"It's a numerical puzzle. You've never solved it before?"

I grabbed yesterday's newspaper (Pelagia instilled the habit of buying newspapers in me, but judging by her mocking giggle, she already possessed that secret knowledge of "reading between the lines" – the activity, which everyone repeated to me about with superiority).

I explained the rules of solving sudoku to Ali briefly.

"It's just numbers," Ali looked at my solved puzzle. "Do you think it's more developing than watching TV?"

"You don't know because you've never solved one."

"I think she had a bit of a screw loose. And in the end, she said that instead of harakiri, she would strangle herself with her scarf so it would be more amusing."

"You have a poor sense of humor, but I think it's the only reason you didn't go crazy. It gave you some distance from the situation."

"After Pelagia's death, I couldn't sleep for a week."

"And you kept your food 20 centimeters away from her body."

"Ala, I'm still stuck in this shit."

"Are you sure someone called you?" Ala checked the phone.

"Well, there was a call in the middle of the night, but you might have misheard it. Maybe you're starting to lose it a bit?"

"Just a moment ago, you announced that our Pelagia had discovered something sensational."

"I think she was a bit off, but quite intelligent."

"Like all psychopaths. Give me that note."

Pelagia had nicely drawn her encryption idea on the paper. I found it to be a pretty useful idea, for example, I could use it to exchange messages with Alicia. If only she could solve sudoku. Another thing is that Pelagia sent this list somewhere, but after some modifications... To simplify the matter, I could solve some random sudoku and give it to Ali as a matrix. We weren't spies, so there was no sudden surveillance threat. Ala could peacefully go to classes with my puzzle.

"This will come in handy. I'll teach you how to use it and we'll be able to use the phone safely."

Alicja quickly caught on to what was going on. We started studying the papers further.

When it comes to anonymous reports, Pelagia could have been called the Queen of Snitches. Written in a clever way, they suggested to the reader that they were written by an uneducated, jealous person.

"Listen to this," we interrupted each other during our reading when we came across a particularly interesting report.

"Mrs. Maria, born as Wroz, I don't know her married name, hit a deer with her car two years ago. The car was fine. The deer died on the spot. Mrs. Maria laughed as she told the story. She said she had roast meat for several weeks. She told the whole village about this story, so there are witnesses like Karol from the Nowak family and Janina from the Dwor family."

"Jack, a businessman from Polna Street, dumps his garbage in the forest. He's so lazy that he has his employees do it for him, so you'll find witnesses."

"Where did she get this information?" Alice wondered.

"It's a shame that such a beautiful and somewhat intelligent woman fell so low as to write anonymous reports. She poked me with her philosophy of optimism. But I think it was just for show. She was a bitter old hag."

"Come on," Ala protested. "I wouldn't let that deer or garbage off the hook either."

"It looks like a noble act, but believe me, I knew her better. Maybe what she writes in those reports isn't true? Notice that she always cites subordinates or friends as witnesses. When they deny it during the investigation, everyone will think they're lying to save their own or the accused's skin."

"Have you ever written a denunciation?"

I briefly told the story about doctor Plonski.

"You're kidding, who would want to do that? He's such a bore. You know what, I'll light up. "

"Are you joking?"

"I smoke from time to time. That's why I sometimes can't control myself. I didn't want you to know about this little addiction of mine. I like you, but after a few hours, all I can think about is lighting up, not listening to your considerations. That's why I'm sometimes so mean. And besides, I'm going on a date tomorrow. Thanks for setting up the account."

Ala lit a cigarette and said she was cold and still had to study for tomorrow's exam and get ready for the date. I made her tea and escorted her downstairs. The ordered taxi looked suspicious, just like the exceptionally handsome taxi driver.

"Take care of yourself," I blurted out.

"Okay, Mom."

I tried to sleep. I made myself a bed in the kitchen, turned up the heating to the max, and snuggled into my down sleeping bag.

Alicia and I agreed that she would let me know what time she would arrive in the morning. I planned to greet anyone who showed up at an unspecified time with a potato masher. When I woke up, it was noon.

And I had only slept for a few hours before continuing to read through the papers. Apparently, even a direct threat couldn't disturb my supernaturally large need for sleep.

There was an SMS waiting for me from Alicja. "I'm giving you the results of the quiz: 1)114 2) 282 3)108 4)292 5)532 6)605 7)445 8)512 9)515 10)134".

I was wondering if such a text would raise suspicion for anyone who took the trouble to read our messages. I decided that they would probably be surprised, but if they attended university, they would just laugh.

I once had a teacher who came up with a very complicated and obviously unfavorable grading method. He added up points and put them into a formula he invented. No one could decipher the secrets of this formula. And even if someone tracking our activities realized that something was wrong, I would have some satisfaction from it.

They shouldn't think it's so easy to beat a student with a "wolf ticket". In fact, I should be proud of that status.

Throughout history, mainly rebellious individuals who later caused revolutions and riots were expelled from universities. I had no such plans. I dreamed of a peaceful, idyllic life as a nerd. Five years of study, then some intellectual work, such as a scientific researcher. I found our code and after a moment, I read Alice's message: "Ala kidnapped."

Raid

The knocking on the door was loud and alarming. Only a stranger could knock like that. And they did it with the audacity that meant they felt entitled to do so. I wasn't mistaken.

"Police! Open up!"

I froze in place. In a split second, I decided to pretend that I wasn't in the apartment. Maybe they'll just leave? After all, they didn't know that I was inside. But they did.

"Open up! We know you're in there! We have a dog!"

So I opened the door.

The first one to enter was a drooling German Shepherd. He jumped at me with his front paws.

Disoriented and unprepared for such a frontal attack, I fell over. Four policemen entered the apartment.

"Where is he? Wildman, find him! Where are you hiding him?"

I was ready for any question, even for an arrest on suspicion of murder. This question caught me off guard. Or was it some psychological game?

"Who?," I asked.

"Don't pretend. We already know everything. Wildman, find him!" one of the policemen commanded the dog. The dog wagged its tail, sniffed the floor, and ran to the bathroom with a strange growl.

Two policemen drew and upholstered their guns. They ran after the dog and with a roar of "POLICE!" they burst into the bathroom. I heard the whining of the German Shepherd. The dog knew what had happened there. The policemen didn't.

"Empty!" shouted one of them. They began running around the apartment, pulling back curtains, looking under the bed and in the closet... When they realized that no one else was in the apartment besides me, they gathered around me as I sat on the floor.

The dog ran out of the bathroom and looked at me with reproach.

"So where is he?" shouted one of the policemen. I didn't know who they were talking about.

"When you remember, report to the station within 24 hours," one of the policemen said in a whisper. They slowly made their way out to the hallway of the tenement. One of them whistled for the dog. The German Shepherd ran up to me, licked my cheek, and then ran out of the apartment.

Feeling terrified, I was even more stressed and relieved at the same time. Stressed because I had to report something within 24 hours without knowing what it was about. The relief came from saying goodbye to Wildman,the dog. Maybe the dog sensed that I wasn't a complete monster, even though I had dissolved someone's body with chemicals.

Or maybe it's a mistake? Maybe the message to report to the police is an attempt to save face in this situation? I decided to act like a "normal person" and file a complaint.

Nobody showed me a search warrant, nobody informed me of my rights. I got up from the floor, drank the glass of water I had prepared in the evening, and dialed the police number on my cell phone.

"Oh, it's you from the dead girl! ... I mean, the missing one!" The duty officer interrupted me when I started introducing myself.

"Dead girl?" I whispered.

"You don't know anything, but it's better if you find another apartment."

"Why?"

"You don't know anything, but the missing girl... how should I put it... was found in the river's current. But I didn't tell you that."

"The police were just here, I'm calling about that..."

"Our guys? And what did they want?"

"They were looking for someone in my apartment and..."

"Who?"

"I don't know…"

"Unfortunately, I'm not authorized to provide such information." The police officer hung up. Who found the drowned girl? And who identified her as Pelagia?

"Enough of the lethargy. It's time to take action. Especially since Alice's life is now at stake, unless it was one of her jokes. I called her phone number. I heard the voicemail. I couldn't believe she was kidnapped. If she was, I couldn't disclose the events to the police. It's likely the killer wanted me to be discreet. Or maybe they wanted something else?

I sat in the kitchen for two hours, waiting for a call from the kidnapper. But no one contacted me. I called Alice again. Again, I only heard her voice on the voicemail.

I decided to act more actively. I got on a tram and went to the only hospital in the city, the memorable one that I escaped from a few weeks ago. The mortuary was in a separate building in the hospital park. The door was closed, and no one responded to my knocking.

I started wandering around the hospital until I stumbled upon the ENT clinic. The woman at the reception looked very bored. Maybe it was my chance? I approached the reception desk."

"What's going on?" asked the receptionist.

"I'm here about the death of my landlady...I'm behind on rent and I'm trying to find her family," I replied.

"I'm sorry, but this is a laryngology clinic," the receptionist said.

"Someone from the family must have identified the body. Could I leave my phone number so someone can pass it on to them?" I asked.

"Are you deaf?" the receptionist blurted out.

"And what if I am? It's very impolite to point out someone's hearing impairment, especially in a clinic like this. What if I file a complaint?" I replied.

"Maybe I'll make an exception," the receptionist said. "After all, honest people like you are rare. Someone else wouldn't admit they haven't paid their rent."

She reached for the phone and dialed a number.

"Helenka? Who identified the latest drowning victim? That woman? Metlicki? Yes, give me his phone number. I'll explain over coffee. Yes, I also have cheesecake..."

After a moment, I held in my hand, of course, the phone number for Jan Metlicki. The same memorable number from which Mrs. Pelagia received a message after her death. I pulled out her cell phone and at that same moment, a call came in from Jan Metlicki, of course. I answered, collapsing on the bench in the clinic.

"You know, who's calling?"

"I know, but I can't say."

"Student pranks... When will they end? I have your ugly girl. If you say anything, she'll disappear. And faster than Pela did. Her date didn't go so well."

"Pela? I'm in a public place."

"You didn't run away with the money, you loser, so now you'll pay it back. And not a peep to the police. And if not, they'll get to you. You had a sample today."

Metlicki hung up.

Overthinking

I wanted to call the police as soon as I picked up the phone. Finally, I would have proof that something was wrong with Metlicki. That he was a cold-blooded killer and kidnapper. But something was holding me back. Ala. Would she survive? Probably not.

I left the hospital and returned to my apartment. On the one hand, I felt immense stress, but on the other hand, relief that I would finally confront the killer.

Even as a victim, it was still a step forward to get out of the awkward situation I had gotten myself into. After all, it was rather impossible for Metlicki, after inheriting Pelagia's apartment, to continue subletting a room to me. It would be against all interactions between murderers and someone who knew about their crimes.

I decided to make Metlicki's life a little more complicated. I called the lawyers who had been calling Pelagia every now and then. While waiting for the call, I remembered our naive thoughts that Ala could pretend to be Pelagia.

"Exactly like children," I said aloud.

"Excuse me?" came a voice through the phone. "Sorry, I was talking about something else. I'm calling about Mrs. Pelagia Metlicka. I wanted to inform you that she's probably dead, at least she hasn't returned from a several-day trip... I'll be meeting with her relatives soon. Would you gentlemen be interested in attending this meeting?"

"Is that Jan Metlicki? Well, you've gotten yourself into a mess. No, we're not interested. He'll eat you for a snack and then wash it down with dry wine. Ha ha!"

The lawyer hung up. I turned on my computer and googled Jan Metlicki's personal information again. This time the computer worked. The first man with that name caught my attention.

A member of parliament, a candidate for the marshal. He used to manage an intelligence agency in the past. Well, the lawyers were probably right.

I wasn't in for anything good in a confrontation with someone like him. The only thing that surprised me was that he hadn't killed me yet.

Maybe he was curious how I would dispose of the body? Or he was like a cat playing with a mouse before delivering the fatal blow... In this situation, I decided not to call the police, not to inform them about Alicia's kidnapping, or about a slightly different version of Pelagia's death. I wanted to patiently wait until the kidnapper came up with some demands, and then obediently fulfill them. I felt like an insignificant gear in one of my robots.

It supposedly contributed to the driving of the entire mechanism, but it was just a piece of metal.

As an individual, I didn't stand a chance. Right from the beginning of this story, I was at a disadvantage, like Sisyphus. And like him, I had little chance of a positive outcome. It would have been different if, like in action movies, I had a pack of well-connected friends.

But that wasn't the case. Only in westerns could one righteous person fight against a gang of thugs. Only in such movies. Life looked very different for a twenty-year-old former student, with a head full of dreams, which were poorly defined and with a huge amount of helplessness.

Nobody taught me to actively participate in my own life. Any excessive activity was punished both at home and at school. I grew up as a tame sheep in a flock, not as a superhero.

What could I do in the current situation besides waiting for the kidnapper's phone call? I decided to occupy myself with something to pass the time and started going through Pelagia's papers.

Was she a secret agent? Or a Russian? Why did she obediently let herself be killed? There were no signs of a struggle. Her diaries were written in very blurry handwriting. I didn't have the inspiration to decipher them.

I focused on her reports. There was no dirt on Jan Metlicki. So what made him kill her? I probably would never find out.

Life is not an action movie where every puzzle piece is discovered by a clever detective. But maybe it would be better for me to live in ignorance? The issue of Alicia remained. Did Metlicki let her go?

It will probably end up with me becoming the lowest category worker in my uncle's processing plant. My dreams of a career will turn into six days of hard work, resting in front of the TV on Sundays, and drinking beer to kill the pain of existence.

But isn't this fate better than serving a sentence for the deeds of politician Metlicki? As if summoned by my thoughts, Metlicki called at the moment when I was imagining stabbing him with a fork in a cafe where I would meet him if he allowed me to.

"The ugly duckling has become even uglier, I don't know if you'll believe it!" Metlicki began the conversation.

"Sir, is that appropriate for your position?"

"I have immunity. So I do what I want. And you, yes, especially you, won't stop me. You're just dust in the wind..."

"I don't read the Bible."

"Are you challenging me? If I don't get my money back, and you don't disappear from this city, it will be over for the ugly girl. Even her uncle has forgotten about her." I laughed involuntarily.

I imagined the lies Ala could have told him.

"I want some proof that Alicia was kidnapped. I saw her just yesterday, and it's not easy to kidnap her."

'That's true,' Metlicki replied. 'Three of my men had to struggle with her. What kind of proof do you want? A finger? Or maybe a whole hand will interest you?'

"But I won't be able to recognize whether it's her finger! Let her talk on the phone!"

"I stay away from that ugly one. She wanted to lecture me too much. You probably overestimate your abilities too."

"Why didn't you kill me?" I dared to ask.

"Ha, ha! Dust in the wind..." Metlicki hung up.

I still didn't know how to get Alicia back. Apparently, Metlicki used some psychological tactics to crush his opponents even before the confrontation. However, my psyche was already sufficiently damaged by the clumsy disposal of Pelagia's body. His games slid off me like oil on baked pepper. I started to ponder this metaphor. Oil on baked food doesn't completely drain off. Part of it soaks into the structure of the food.

Presumably, his psychological games also left some mark, a crack in my psyche. I had enough of everything. Prison didn't matter to me, only my uncle Henek's processing plant scared me with its inevitability.

Metlicki called in the evening.

"Tomorrow in the café where you met Pelagia. You have to come alone, not inform anyone, and bring the money."

"With Pelagia's diaries too?" I asked.

"No one will read them, damn it, don't piss me off," Metlicki replied.

"At what time?" I asked.

Metlicki gave me the time and hung up.

I searched the entire apartment for more bundles of banknotes. In total, I found 150,000 zlotys. Most of it was in Pelagia's dresser, where she had hidden the money, wrapping it in her old panties.

Fortunately, they were washed. The meeting was scheduled for tomorrow. Knowing I wouldn't be able to sleep, I made myself a strong cup of coffee.

My entire life flashed before my eyes. I wondered if this was the end of my unsuccessful life, and it made me even more reluctant to sleep. The café opened at nine in the morning.

Meeting

Several women dressed in black were already sitting in the café when I arrived. I sat down at an empty table.

"What kind of mourning convention is this?" A voice reached me.

I turned around. Metlicki was standing behind me. Where did he come from? How could I not notice him? Did he come out from behind the counter?

I pulled out the bag with the money towards him.

"Calm down, I don't have the goods yet," he waved his hand. He seemed slightly nervous, which didn't fit his previous confidence.

"So that's what you call her?" I protested.

"Like everyone else!" he replied.

"She's not too pretty, as you know..."

"That's the traditional name. Goods are goods."

"I don't know. It's my first time when..."

"What will you drink?" Metlicki interrupted me.

"Nothing, thank you."

I remembered the lack of a fight before Pelagia's death. Maybe that bastard had given her something?

Two guys walked into the café. One of them had a mustache, and the other looked similar to one of the policemen who raided my apartment. Maybe they're looking for me now? After all, I had something to report to the police, but why bother?

"Do you need regular deliveries?" Metlicki's voice reached me.

"I don't understand."

"Will this delivery be enough for you? Students like to experiment..."

"What do you mean?"

"Take out the cash, or you'll never see the goods again."

I obediently took out the bag full of money. Metlicki put his folder on the table. He winked at me and pulled out some packets wrapped in newspaper.

I barely remember the rest.

Two guys jumped up from the neighboring table and shouted "Police!" They ran towards me.

After a moment, already in handcuffs, I watched as one of them unfolded a newspaper. Hidden underneath it was a packet of white powder.

A heavy weight stuck in my chest. I tried to breathe, but my lungs felt like they weighed a ton. Desperately, I tried to catch my breath. Seeing this, one of the policemen hit me.

The pain in my tooth where his fist had made contact sobered me up a bit.

"He's holding... he's holding..."

"No more product for you, you drug addict scum!" interrupted Metlicki, hitting the same spot as the policeman with an open hand.

The mustached one began reading me my rights, while taking pictures at the same time.

"Gentlemen, calm down. There are industrial cameras here," Metlicki reassured them.

I fell silent. I preferred not to speak and leave it to my lawyer. I didn't know that the lawyer assigned to me would also remain silent. She remained obstinately silent at all the trials, previously saying that I should not speak up.

I remained silent. She remained silent. The prosecutors tormented me. Nobody mentioned Pelagia with a word.

I wondered if I should tell the whole story. However, I remembered the incident with Dr. Płoński. Nobody believed me when I told them about him. Not even Alicia, who disappeared without a trace. I wondered what could have happened to her. Did she run away? Was she killed in a scuffle with Metlicki's thugs?

Or perhaps taken down as an inconvenient witness?

During subsequent trials, thousands of words raced through my head. They aimed for a five-year sentence, as there was no other evidence besides the attempt to sell the "merchandise", which turned out to be Metlicki's cocaine.

On one of the trials, Metlicki himself told the story of how I harassed him, threatening to expose his affair, which I found out about from Pelagia's papers, unless he sold me his merchandise.

"Why did the defendant think that Mr. Jan Metlicki had any merchandise?" the judge asked me, who seemed slightly disoriented by the whole situation. I saw fear in her eyes. Apparently, she didn't want to know my truth.

I was about to speak up, but my lawyer preempted me:

"The defendant has nothing to say!"

While sitting in detention, I did some quick calculations. For murder or concealing a murder, I faced a lot more years behind bars. So maybe it was better to follow my lawyer's advice and stay silent?

Metlicki seemed to be running this town. How was it possible that I hadn't heard about him before? Why did I end up crossing him?

During the transport to the courtroom, I saw how nature was coming back to life. Spring had arrived. My first spring behind bars.

In prison, I learned how to fight. I didn't have a choice, or rather the choice was bleak – either get beaten up or only partially beaten up. I preferred a few blows to several hundred. At first, I curled up, trying to protect my poor head – I still believed in its potential – from further blows. However, when they didn't stop, I finally decided to fight back someday. That's how my nightly brawls with other inmates began, who couldn't tolerate drug dealers. It's a good thing they didn't know that I dissolved the old lady's body; each of them talked about their love for their own grandmother.

My fights didn't bode well for my sentence. Like stocks on the exchange, it fluctuate every time, sometimes up, sometimes down. It ended up being three years. The only thing that comforted me was that for three years, I would be spared from working in my uncle's processing plant. But what happened to Alicia? Did she share Pelagia's fate? I had no idea what was happening outside the cell.

My parents only visited me once.

"I was set up. I can't say more," I tried to convince them of my innocence, but I saw disappointment in their eyes and a slight disgust.

"Son, why the drugs! You were so smart! You could even construct robots!"

From that day on, robots started to appear in my dreams every day. There were dreams with robots – lawyers, robots – cops, robots – fellow inmates.

I woke up covered in sweat, which convinced my fellow prisoners that I was going through physical withdrawal from drugs.

I asked to meet with a psychologist. I told them about my dreams of robots and asked if I could make a model under supervision that could be sold for charity. Maybe it would help me disconnect from my nightmares.

"Maybe it can be arranged in prison," the psychologist replied.

However, getting permission in prison was not easy at all.

Prison

In prison, I was put in a cell with some lunatic. He never slept, wandered around at night, and when he finally slept in the morning, he talked in his sleep. He also hated drug dealers.

He was a physical development enthusiast and exercised for several hours every day, which gave me a headache because the smell of his sweat filled the cell. Drugs were something very, very bad for him. He ended up in prison for some unknown crime, probably murder, as he had several years left to serve.

I immediately told him that I was framed for drugs and didn't confess because my acquaintance was kidnapped.

"Bullshit!" he interrupted me. "You'll get beaten up anyway." And I did.

I called him a lunatic, but I probably wasn't any better. I kept dreaming about robots. I woke up covered in sweat. I signed up for a tinkering workshop. I was slightly annoyed by the personal searches after the classes. They thoroughly checked whether anyone was taking any materials from the workshops.

Spring has passed. The summer came hot, and there was no air conditioning in the prison. After all, it wasn't a hotel. However, some thought otherwise and complained about the food, boredom, and overall hopelessness. I lived in a cell facing south, so the heat affected us more. Just like the smell of sweat after my cellmate's exercises. He was relentless. He exercised for four hours every day.

"How can you exercise like that?" I started a conversation one day.

"Am I a woman? I don't have my period, so I can exercise every day. Have you had any news about your kidnapped friend?"

"No," I sighed. I must have had a genuinely sad face because he suddenly believed me.

"What was that story anyway?"

"I can't say."

"Do you have any plans at all?" he asked.

"Plan? For what?"

"Because I'm planning what I'm going to do after I get out..."

I was at a loss for words. The guy had seventeen more years to serve. What could he plan? On the other hand, maybe that was the only thing keeping him sane?

"You're getting out in three years and eleven months? And you don't plan anything?" he asked in surprise.

Apparently, we thought completely differently. I started to feed on his hope, and he, finding a loyal listener in me, began to tell me in detail what he would do after getting out.

He would open a sports clothing wholesale store. Or a sports shop. Or a gym. In addition, he would open a fast food chain. He was spinning so many business opening plans that one day I risked asking a question.

"Where will you get the money for that?"

My cellmate chuckled.

"How come! From you. After all, you'll be set up in three years without a month. When I get out in seventeen years, you'll already be set, won't you?"

Suddenly, he jumped out of his bunk and thrust his fist under my nose. A razor blade stuck out from between his fingers.

I felt a sudden trickle of sweat running down my spine.

"Ha! Ha!" He laughed and went back to his place.

I was silent, horrified. He could have just as easily slit my throat with that razor blade. I had been somewhat seasoned in fights after the arrest, but not at a master level yet.

"So, what's it gonna be? Will you help your friend?"

"Yes, of course!"

"Don't bullshit me!"

He jumped out of his bunk again.

"Do you think I'm stupid? Tell me how you'll earn that money!"

"I'll sell robots."

I knew that life in prison wouldn't be a picnic, but I never expected to have to write a business plan here. That's what my cellmate, who went by the name Razorblade, demanded of me. Now I knew roughly how he came to be the owner of that nickname.

My stories about selling robots gave him some hope, but he didn't just want to listen, he wanted me to act.

At first, I wanted to complain. I arranged a visit with the prison psychologist, who didn't let me get a word in and said he didn't want any complaints about fellow inmates because it made his job more complicated, that he didn't want any imaginary illnesses because medical doctors handle those cases, and that if I came with something else he'd consider helping me.

"This is related to forbidden topics. I need to construct a few robots," I said.

The psychologist's already bulging eyes widened. He looked at me like a rarely seen specimen of a species threatened with extinction.

"Robots..." he repeated.

"My life depends on it, but I can't describe why, because you told me not to talk about it."

"What kind of robots?"

"Small ones that move from time to time using self-propelling mechanisms."

"Without batteries?"

"Correct."

"Do you need weapons?"

"Are you selling weapons?" This time, I must have looked dumbfounded.

"Robots... I'll see what I can do. I'd like to have the prettiest robot on my shelf."

"What do you mean by the prettiest?"

"Just as you understood it. The prettiest. If it's ugly, I'll cut short your fantasies a bit."

I returned to my cell feeling down. None of my robots were beautiful. They were beautiful to me, if a screw here and there protruded when the joints were accentuated, but would anyone understand that?

"Did you set me up?" Razor was exercising his abs.

"Maybe I can start production. It all depends on the psychologist, and he wants the prettiest robot for himself."

"What's the problem?"

"They're pretty, but I don't know if they'll be for him."

"So, you'll make something for him, right? Life's school, life's school. I'll teach you to stop selling drugs."

I tried to hide under my blanket. I felt like crying. So even my beloved hobby would be tainted by the whims of others. Razor interrupted his exercises. He walked over to my bed and pulled off the blanket.

"What's the point of making robots if you're going to collapse later?"

"What do you mean?"

"You're not exercising at all! Man, you're going to drop like a fly, and soon. I'll make a man out of you, you'll see."

That's how my unusual torment began. I was forced to exercise muscles that I never knew existed, but now I felt that I did have them, and since they hadn't been used in a long time, they did indeed hurt.

Razor didn't let up on me. I had to exercise for two and a half hours every day. Luckily, he exercised on his own for the next two and a half hours. I wanted to change my cellmate, but it wasn't easy.

Besides, who knows what other lunatic I would have ended up with?

So I exercised every day, pretending that it gave me pleasure. The muscle soreness didn't go away, and I walked around more and more stiff and sore.

Meanwhile, the psychologist seemed to have gotten a little crazy after my story about the robots, as he provided me with materials for a few pieces.

All the prisoners present at the workshop mocked me as they saw me tinkering with a pile of screws and pieces of metal.

However, when they saw the first leg of the robot, they fell silent. They gathered around me, including the workshop leader, and I felt their breath on my neck.

The robot had to be created, as I couldn't expect more intimate conditions for creating it in a place like prison.

The first robot was snatched from my hands as soon as I tightened the last screw. The prisoner who was watching it almost had a heart attack when the robot suddenly moved its arm.

Others recoiled and then started laughing hysterically. I became the star of the day. The problem was that I was supposed to show the first robot to Razorblade, give it to the psychologist, but suddenly a chain of eager owners formed.

The news reached the prison director, who took the robot to his office under the guise of empirical research. I thought my prison life would end there. Razorblade would beat me up, and the psychologist would say I did it myself out of revenge. I would end up in some strange unit where the crazies would deal with me in an unkind way. However, things turned out differently...

Journalist

On that day, a well-known journalist visited the prison to conduct an interview about the rehabilitation of prisoners in the Polish prison system. The interview was supposed to take place in the director's office.

The office had a somewhat unusual appearance - on the shelves were jars of pickled cucumbers and traditionally preserved mushrooms. The director was afraid that due to excessive stress, he would suffer from some civilization disease. He had read somewhere about the beneficial effects of fermented foods and ate them daily, even though he didn't like their taste.

The journalist wouldn't be a journalist if she didn't ask about them. The fifty-seven jars were too noticeable not to inquire.

Taken aback by the question about his fermented foods, the director rolled his eyes in confusion and his gaze landed on my robot.

"Madam, you wanted to talk about rehabilitation... Here we have a robot made by one of the prisoners. It's a prototype."

"And what can this robot do?" The journalist grimaced at the sight of the little figure I had made. The prison director placed the robot on his desk.

"Every now and then they move. They have some kind of self-propelling mechanism inside. And they don't need batteries..."

"Wouldn't it be better to make them wind-up?" the journalist asked.

"And how does this relate to rehabilitation? There's a factory nearby, why aren't the prisoners working there?"

"We're thinking about it, but the legal system doesn't allow for slavery. The prisoners would have to receive compensation."

"That's volunteer work. And points for good behavior. Haven't you thought about that? Let them produce robots for example."

"And who's going to buy that?"

"You already did, since it's on your shelf with the pickles. Speaking of pickles, what are they doing here?"

The poor director didn't know which topic was worse. To satisfy the journalist's hunger for a story that could make the front page, he called me into his office to explain how well my rehabilitation was going.

It wasn't going very well. I was summoned to the office at the last minute. Razorblade went into a rage when he found out that the robot prototype had been taken. I showed up in the office with a bruised eye.

The journalist decided to mock me.

"You have nice makeup, do you do it every day?" she said.

I had had enough and decided not to be pushed around. The status of the prisoner obligated me to something. I didn't have to be a nice guy who escorts old ladies across the street. I dissolved those old ladies in caustic soda.

"With makeup or without, I definitely look better than you," I said. "If I hadn't seen you on TV before, I would have thought it was the apocalypse with a zombie as the lead."

"Great ... I see that unemployment is not good for you," she said. "Have you ever worked?"

"At my uncle's factory," I replied.

"And you said you would bring a robot expert, but you brought a wax figure maker," the journalist complained to the director.

"You're stupid," the director replied. The journalist muttered under her breath.

Apparently, she wanted to slam the door and leave, but she didn't have all the data for her article yet.

"Decide whether you want to write about wax figures or robots," the director said.

"I'll write about both," the journalist replied.

She turned around at the door and showed us the middle finger.

"These are the standards nowadays," the director sighed. Before I left, he told me to describe the method of creating robots and to improve them by making them wind-up.

The only thing I gained from it was that Razorblade left me alone. The psychologist didn't know about the whole affair yet. He found out the next day from the front page of the newspaper.

"Instead of getting to work, prisoners produce robots" read the title of the article. Below were speculations about legal procedures to force prisoners to work systematically. The journalist didn't speak very highly of the director, calling him a "madman of the Jars era", "not controlling what was happening in his prison".

Somehow, the journalist managed to snap a photo of the robot. And that's when it started.

At first, one phone call. Then another. By the end of the day, both the director's landline and cell phone were ringing non-stop. Everyone wanted a robot made by the "murderer", as I was called in the article.

The director initially explained that I wasn't a murderer, that no, it wasn't for sale. After a few hours, he began taking orders, not yet knowing how to handle it legally. A lawyer came to the rescue. They decided to set up a foundation, with the proceeds going towards psychological help for victims of crime. Of course, some money was to be kept for the foundation's management. We didn't know anything about it. We became the director's slaves. Of course, we worked voluntarily to earn proverbial points for good behavior.

The director cut off access to television, under the pretext of its negative influence on prisoners, and only played children's cartoons.

This way we didn't know how much of a sensation our, or rather my, robots were causing outside the prison walls. Even visits to our ward were forbidden for the prisoners.

The director only failed to foresee one thing. As a naive eighteen-year-old, I patented my robots. At the time, I thought they would sell themselves. I didn't know that a story was also needed - the darker, the better, in this case, murderers producing toys.

The human psyche will forever remain a mystery to me. For now, I only suspected that someone was making a lot of money off me. I wrote down on pieces of paper the number of robots produced each day. We made more and more of them. Finally, the director decided to rent a production line from a nearby factory. Thanks to this, Alice was freed.

Escape

Razorblade eventually took a job in robot production. He was slacking off terribly. More often than not, he could be seen chatting with the warehouse workers. I didn't know what they could be talking about. Used to his appearing and disappearing at the production line, we didn't notice when one day at the end of the shift, he took off.

He vanished into thin air. During the investigation, it turned out, as rumors had it, that the day before he had asked for new shoes, and even earlier had bought pepper. Apparently for bland food.

The prisoners speculated that he did it to throw off the hounds. The interrogated warehouse workers explained that he often asked them for the opportunity to nap, because he lived with a terribly snoring and sleep-talking guy - meaning me. On the one hand, I was relieved by Razorblade's escape, but on the other hand, I was afraid for my family's fate. Would he not pay them an unexpected visit? He extracted all information from me, addresses, descriptions...

I thought he would stay in prison for another 17 years and forget about my loved ones. That's why I liked to talk about my mom's soup she makes on Mondays, and how my dad spends his time after work. Razorblade heard so many stories about Uncle Henrik's cannery that he sometimes interrupted me, saying, "Don't worry, you're in prison, you don't have to work there."

From time to time, he asked about Alicia. What does she look like exactly? Is she really that ugly, and does she really have such a slender and well-groomed body? A few weeks after his escape, I received a postcard. It was unsigned, with only a short message: "Greetings and thanks. Ala."

I turned the postcard over to check the picture. It depicted a woman standing in front of a large train station. I looked closer. That woman was Alicia! She was holding a package of razors in her hand. The date on the station clock behind her showed it was from two weeks ago. Alicia looked healthy. From what I could see, she wasn't missing any limbs.

How did this whole affair unfold? Did Metlicki release her after putting me in prison? Or did Razorblade, like a superhero, set her free? And hence the package of razors, to remind me of a new debt of gratitude?

I was overjoyed. My face, beaming with happiness, aroused suspicion among the prison guards and they rushed over with some papers to check for any traces of drugs on my body. I also had to provide a blood and urine sample. So, Ala is free now. But should I be happy about it? I couldn't really count on her discretion. The most discreet are the dead, like Pelagia. And is Ala safe now? My euphoria dimmed.

A few weeks later, another postcard arrived, showing only best grades on a report card. The owner of the report card was Alicia. So, her life was now back to normal. She attended classes, maybe she was never even abducted? But what if she really wasn't kidnapped?

However, I didn't curse my fate. Apparently, it was meant to be. I deserved penance from life for getting rid of Pelagia's body. Besides, I had stumbled into a blind alley and didn't know how to get out of it.

After Razorblade's escape, I was missing something and felt very bad. Soon, I discovered that it was the lack of physical exercise that had so badly affected my well-being. I stopped doing them immediately after my cellmate's escape.

The new guy was a lawyer. He seemed very intelligent, sly, and I couldn't for the life of me understand how he got caught up in his own schemes. As it turned out, his client betrayed him for unknown reasons, because he himself had to explain himself for following the lawyer's eccentric and very creatively legal advice. We didn't know what to call him, so we just called him Lawyer.

The lawyer was looking for an ally in the tough prison conditions. He was thin, tall, and weak. His weapon was definitely his mind, but that wasn't the best asset in prison.

Naturally, it fell to me to become his buddy since we shared a cell. He started telling me about his scams and plans, how he intends to legally leave this prison within six months.

"Don't you want to get out soon?" he asked me once.

"I like not having to cook. I'm staying," I joked, since the food in prison was not a five-star delicacy. Michelin avoided this place, only Sanitary Inspection came often with visits and then we starved because the kitchen was closed every time.

The lawyer soon found out that I was the author of the robots. As a newcomer to prison, he knew perfectly well the sensation they caused outside the prison walls. The factory workers mentioned something, but I thought it was a joke.

"I patented them, I'll get back what was taken from me," I said once when I couldn't take his insults about using me as an idea generator anymore.

I thought I would have peace, but it had only just begun.

The lawyer laid out legal methods for me to regain the rights to all the money received by the foundation for the robots. He effortlessly spouted legal loopholes and managed to get paper and records from other lawyers, noting article numbers and various annotations he could use to his advantage. He seemed to know every legal statute by heart.

However, as a weakling, he didn't gain much popularity in prison. I told him to start exercising, just 15 minutes a day at first. When the other inmates saw him working out, they left him alone and started asking him for advice on their own legal troubles.

Soon we were living like kings, with the lawyer getting anything he wanted in exchange for his legal advice. Despite the fact that I could potentially make millions from my robots in the future, I wasn't as popular and had to participate in fights to maintain my dignity and avoid falling to the bottom of the social ladder in prison.

My parents didn't visit me, especially after I became famous as the murderer who created the robots. I felt that I could have even bigger problems after being released with that reputation, and all doors seemed to be closing in front of me. But that didn't happen.

The lawyer became my friend, maybe the first real friend I've ever had. Before, I mostly had girlfriends, maybe for the wrong reasons, maybe not. He was released a few months before me and managed to come up with a strategy to reclaim the money taken by the prison director, free of charge.

When I finally got released from prison, six months earlier for good behavior, the Lawyer had already prepared all the papers. All his brilliance, notifying the media about the case, and of course the patent, made me very wealthy. And then I discovered that I didn't have to worry about my prison reputation. Money opened all the doors for me.

Please review this book

If you would like to read more from K. E. Adamus

here is the link to her short stories compilation,
Losers

www.ingramcontent.com/pod-product-compliance
Lightning Source LLC
Chambersburg PA
CBHW050355260626
47156CB00003B/739